# THE NANNY JOB

## BITE-SIZED JOBS BOOK 2

### EVE LANGLAIS

CHAPTER ONE

THE GOBLIN LAY STRETCHED on the rack, four limbs strapped. Ungagged for the moment. Ugly creature. A simple-minded minion. Easy to find and cheap to hire.

"Who's paying you?" Frederick asked, because goblins didn't act of their own volition. They preferred to hide in the underground, the sewers being considered their domain.

The creature grinned, showing off cracked and yellowing teeth. "Your mother sucks dick."

His mother—rest her miserable god-loving soul —didn't suck, lick, or enjoy anything to do with sex. Frederick unfortunately knew this because his father used to complain she'd barely part her legs.

A pious woman didn't enjoy sex, at least not in the century of his birth.

While Frederick missed the fresh air and open spaces of those days, he didn't lament the lack of modern amenities. Hot water and indoor toilets being some of his favorites.

"It occurs to me that we could spend some time bantering back and forth. Me demanding answers. You spouting off some stupid shit meant to make me mad." A lie actually. As if a man his age got angry so easily. He'd seen it all. Done it all. Indulged in every argument. Climbed mountains and crossed seas.

During that time, Frederick had encountered many people—and creatures. He knew exactly how things would go with the goblin, and being a man who hated repeating himself uselessly, he'd evolved better methods to deal with reluctant prisoners.

Frederick flicked the power button on a remote and a massive television turned on. One hundred and four inches of sleek LCD. A beauty. Too big for most rooms. The clarity on it rendered in stunning detail.

"Gonna put some porn on?" The goblin leered and licked its bulbous lower lip. A seriously unattractive race. It was why you didn't see many goblin hybrids. Humans tended to have babies with the prettier supernatural species.

Frederick set the remote down. The screen flashed its introductory logos. "There are so many ways to torture, you know. I grew up in a time where we indulged in the messy kind with blood and guts. Delicious when dealing with humans." He did so enjoy a fresh vein and warm skin to latch onto. Sweet, warm, bloody goodness. "But your kind"—Frederick eyed the goblin—"are rather rancid to the taste." Not to mention the stink never came out of anything their fluids touched.

"Kill me and another will come. We'll keep coming and coming." It cackled. It also told the truth.

The bounty on Frederick's head had more than doubled recently. Flattering given it was over twenty million. Could he get it to fifty? He was already tempted to turn himself in for the prize.

"Were you not paying attention to what I said? I'm not going to kill you, but I will send a message to your friends. Your family. And anyone else that's thinking of fucking with me." Frederick smiled. "Did you know that the biggest reason your kind can't live with humans is because of your looks? If you're going to be different, then it needs to be cute. Humans love cute things." Which might be why none of them had ever loved Frederick. No one would ever accuse him of being soft and cuddly.

On the screen, an image appeared. A circle of children with happy faces. Obviously laughing. Then a small video where you could clearly see them singing and dancing. The sound spilled from the speakers softly at first. A distant giggle then the drone-like hum of many voices singing.

*"Ring around the rosy..."* Cute the first few times. After the five hundredth? He'd leave before it got stuck in his head.

"Are you ready for your makeover?" Frederick asked as he headed for the door.

"What?"

"I'm going to make you adorable for the humans."

"You can't do that. I'm hideous," the creature babbled quickly, spitting the words. The goblin lost all cockiness.

"Fear not, my ugly friend. My team can perform miracles." The artists entered, bearing their tools of the trade.

As the nail technician tackled those claws, the pictures kept flipping. A basket of kittens. A video of pomskies. Everything overly adorable. Super sweet. Frederick couldn't watch for too long or he got an urge to do something philanthropic. Last time, his local hospital's children's wing found itself the recipient of a large, anonymous donation.

"Stop. Don't touch my nails," the goblin squealed. "I'll tell you everything. It's the Fae. They hired me."

Frederick snorted. "You're going to have to do better than that because I already knew the Fae hired you. I want a name."

"I don't know their name."

"That's a shame because it means you're going to have to be the example that's going to make it harder for them to hire anyone competent without raising that price." Maybe he could get the bounty on his head to fifty million. A respectable sum for a man of his skills.

"I'll be an outcast!"

"Then tell me something I don't know." Or by the end of the conditioning, the goblin would return a new creature, something the humans would all want. He'd be desired. Cute. His people would be horrified. The goblin would be shunned. The most horrible thing it could conceive of.

It screamed and begged for death. Then told Frederick where he could put a broom handle.

Frederick shut the door on the yelling. A man in his position learned long ago not to hear it. This was simply business. The Fae sent assassins, and Frederick handled them. He handled them so well the Fae appeared reduced to sending morons. This last one never even posed a challenge.

Frederick headed up to the main levels of his chateaux—a grand thing of stone, copied off one he'd seen in Europe but with proper electrical and plumbing. It cost a fortune back in the sixties to build.

Worth every penny and now one of the most expensive and exclusive properties in the world.

He paused and enjoyed the streaming sunlight coming through an unshuttered window. The only vampire in the world who could tolerate it because of a serum given to him by a brilliant man.

Anthony Savell. A scientist who found a way to turn off Frederick's vampire gene when in the presence of UV light. No more fearing he'd melt like a witch. Now he could stand naked in it and get a tan—which he'd done a few times. There was a terrifying thrill in defying the sun he'd feared for so long.

But he couldn't be too blasé about it. The serum required reapplication, as the result didn't last forever. Less than nine days by last count. At least he had warning before it wore off. His skin, no matter how tanned, lost all color. An easy sign, which he paid attention to.

As Frederick neared his office, his secretary—a male with reddish hair in a cockscomb, a snazzy vest paired with a bowtie, and plaid trousers—glanced up from his computer.

Julian held up a finger and said in his microphone headset, "Could you hold for just a moment while I check and see if Mr. Thibodeaux is in?"

Frederick frowned. "Who is that?" Because usually those calling his main office line had a message taken by Julian, who knew which ones to pass along.

The oddest expression tugged at Julian's face. "Sir, it's St. Mary's Hospital."

"Did one of our employees get into trouble?" Frederick asked. Hiring hot-headed Lycans meant you came to expect brawls and other incidents.

"Not exactly. It's...um...probably a hoax?" Julian dodged a real answer, and his voice lifted an octave. Strange, as the man was usually quite composed.

"What's a hoax? You're going to have to explain a bit better." What had Julian so flustered?

"You should hear for yourself, sir." Julian clicked to activate the speaker for his phone and said, "Ma'am, I'm going to pass the phone now to Mr. Thibodeaux."

What? He took the proffered handset and said, "Hello. Thibodeaux here. How can I help you?"

"Hello, sir. I'm Jane Henderson. I work in the offices for St. Mary Hospital."

He cut to the chase. "Why are you calling?"

"To congratulate you on the birth of your daughter."

CHAPTER TWO

HAD HE BEEN HUMAN, Frederick might have hit the floor in a faint, but vampires couldn't have babies. Utterly preposterous. Someone was screwing with him by making the assertion. "Whoever claimed I was the father lied to you."

"Perhaps. A DNA test will clear that up quickly if that's the case. But in the meantime, we have to go with the assumption the female-presenting child, born two hours ago, is yours."

"You'd be wasting a test. It can't be mine." He'd long ago resigned himself to the fact he'd never have a traditional heir.

"I assure you, Mr. Thibodeaux, that I would never have called if there was another choice. But I have to follow rules. Are you sure you don't remember the mother? She mentioned something about the beach and piña coladas."

The words froze him. He never drank umbrella drinks. Except for once. The first time he'd used Anthony's serum.

"Is the child full term?" he suddenly asked. Human gestation was just under ten months. And it had been over nine months ago since the first time he took the cure.

He still remembered that day. Heart in his throat, for the first time in forever, Frederick had walked into the sun, terrified he'd made a mistake. Expecting to burst into flames and hit the ground in a steaming pile of goo.

Step after step, he cringed until he realized the heat on his skin wasn't flames. Once he realized he wouldn't die, he'd run, skipping in the sunlight, giddy with joy.

Yes, giddy.

Not one of his finer moments, and he was happy he never came across any footage of him acting so out of character. His staff would have never let him live it down.

That entire day he'd behaved the opposite of

his usually staid self. He'd frolicked in the sun. And he wasn't alone.

"She's full term by all indications. A big, healthy girl at ten pounds, three ounces," said Jane Henderson.

He had no idea what that signified but began to get a fluttery feeling in his gut. Could it be possible?

After all, it was after that one time that he found out his cure came with one major caveat. While daylight touched him, Frederick was, for all intents and purposes, human. A fragile, easily broken human. He could be run over by a car. Shot. Knifed. Beheaded. The last, he should add, would kill him no matter what.

However, his susceptibility to injury wasn't the only issue when under certain UV circumstances. Forget controlling minds. No one could hear him demanding obedience. He didn't enjoy super strength or vision.

He was weak.

On the flip side, he could eat and drink. Get wasted, as a matter of fact.

That first day of sunlight freedom, he'd gone to the beach and run into the waves. Drank all the margaritas he could find.

Flirted.

Oh, how he flirted, and in the sun, on the sand, behind an outcrop of rock, he'd fucked. Fucked a woman who'd smiled coyly at him as she sipped something frothy. He'd made fun of it and she'd dared him to have a sip of her piña colada.

They hit it off and did what men and women do.

Before night fell, they parted ways. Him smiling all the way home. Only to curse and yell when he found out the truth.

The serum that let him daywalk made him human in all ways, including viable sperm. Surely that one time in the sand wouldn't cause a problem.

"Did she mention how she knew my name?" Because that night, they'd jokingly called themselves Piña for her and Colada for him. They never exchanged true names, addresses, or even a phone number.

Had they, Frederick would have probably lied. His name was too well known. The Frederick Thibodeaux the world knew about had many faces: crime kingpin, a founding family of the city, and master vampire who hid from the humans in plain sight, not someone you fucked with.

"If you really don't want to be tested, we can't make you," Jane Henderson stated.

"It's possible. I'm just having a hard time placing her name. But I keep seeing her bouncy blonde curls."

"Coralline Blenny Starfish."

Now there was a mouthful that didn't rhyme well together. He'd also never heard the name before. "Do you have a picture?"

"No. Ms. Starfish didn't come in with any identification."

Meaning she might have used Frederick's name in the hopes of getting a free ride when it came to costs. It might not be the same woman at all.

But what if...? "We could clear this up quickly if you sent me a picture." Then he could put this strange fantasy of him being a father to rest.

"I can't. I'm sorry to say Ms. Starfish died delivering your daughter."

"How?" Back in his day, women died often in childbirth, but not in this century with modern medicine.

"Gunshot wound. She arrived in the ER injured and in labor. It proved too much for her body. She told us you were the father before she died." The woman hesitated before adding, "She also demanded you not be told. However, state law dictates that, as you're the child's next closest relative, you must be notified."

"What happens if the child isn't mine?" he asked.

"Social services will take over and contact family to see if there are other candidates."

'She'll go into an orphanage?" The idea left a sour taste.

"More like a foster home until we can be sure no one is coming forth to claim her. Then she'll be placed for adoption."

She couldn't be his. Even if she was, he didn't want a child. He'd come to that decision a long time ago.

He'd spent three hundred years—more or less —alone, with only occasional female companionship. None lasted. None could have given him a family. Nor did he want one. If Frederick needed family, he bit someone.

But according to this hospital worker on the phone, he'd possibly created an heir the old-fashioned way.

Could he actually have a daughter? "How soon can I do the DNA test?"

"If you come to the hospital, we can handle it. After all, we'll want to ensure only a true family member gets custody."

"You'd give the child to me?" The very idea flabbergasted. A vampire couldn't raise a human baby.

Then again, what if the girl wasn't human?

*What if the baby is mine and takes after me?*

"I want to see the child."

"Of course, sir. Visiting hours are from nine until seven."

As if those kinds of things applied to him. Entrance only ever required the right price. "I'll be in shortly."

The moment Frederick hung up he placed a call.

The other end was picked up with a drawled, "If it isn't the semi-walking undead."

"Lexie, always a delight to hear your voice." Not entirely true. While there was a time verbally sparring and spying on her helped him jerk off, since she'd mated a geek turned alpha wolf mix, Frederick had to dial it back. One did not hit on married women because even he had lines he wouldn't cross. Not to mention Anthony would literally tear off his dick.

"What do you want? Kind of busy with security detail for my mate, you know." Lexie handled keeping her celebrity scientist safe. Anthony was in the process of revolutionizing the medical field. He'd found a way to heighten healing in people and was currently going through the steps to have it approved. There were factions, especially those in pharmaceuticals, who didn't want him to succeed.

"I need to speak to Anthony," Frederick demanded.

"He's busy."

"You'll both want to hear this."

The line on the other end shifted as she put him on speaker. "Anthony's listening with me. What's happened?"

"The hospital just called. Apparently, I have a newborn daughter."

## CHAPTER THREE

DEAD SILENCE.

"Are you fucking with us?" Lexie growled. "Because that isn't funny." Lexie didn't have a high opinion of Frederick. Not that it ever stopped her from taking the money he paid her for odd jobs.

Anthony took him seriously. "Fred wouldn't have called if he didn't think it worth checking."

"Even if he did manage to knock someone up, a vampire can't raise a human baby." Lexie didn't care Frederick was listening.

"Why not?" Anthony argued. "We both know that monsters raise children all the time and how many of them call themselves human."

"On this, I have to agree with Lexie. I don't

know what to do with a child, and I doubt it's mine. It was only once." Could it have borne fruit?

"It only takes one time," Anthony ominously noted.

"I refuse to believe it." Frederick had only just been transformed. How could his swimmers have become viable that quickly? No. Impossible. The mother must have seen his name and thrown it out there as a possible cash grab for the baby when she knew she might die.

"Does this mean you don't want me testing samples from the child?" Anthony bluntly asked.

Frederick gnashed his teeth. "Of course, I want you to test her. Meet me at the hospital within the hour. Let's settle this."

The sun shone, but Frederick didn't worry. He'd recently taken a serum booster. The sun wouldn't hurt him, but being out and about during the day had its own risks. If his enemies were to discover he could leave his mansion when the sun was out, he might be subject to attack.

Aware of this danger, he'd taken extra precautions since his first wild day at the beach. He enjoyed his sunlight furtively through open windows or by slipping out unnoticed by the watchers.

There was usually a pair of eyes on every gate. Plus one of the recently hired kitchen staff was spying on him. He enjoyed feeding the fellow false information.

Like now. Going for a nap. Expecting guests for dinner.

The kitchen would go in full berserk mode getting ready. Keeping his spy occupied.

Next, Frederick tapped a code into his phone. He met up with his security detail in the garage. Four women, two men. All Lycan. Dressed in black combat pants and shirts. Slick looking, and the credit went to the new guy in charge, Braedan. He'd coordinate from the office. Sasha and Bec would be Frederick's chauffeur and bodyguard today, while the two other pairs would act as decoys.

Having entered the garage via the house, and the windows shuttered against outside eyes, no one could see what went on. Had no idea who sat in the cars.

Behind tinted windows, Frederick remained unseen by prying eyes as the three identical Town Cars left at once and split off in three directions once past the main gates. It sent the watchers scrambling. Sasha ensured they lost their tail and took an extra five minutes of precaution before heading for the hospital.

During that drive, the UV light, strongly filtered through the glass of the car, struck him and his cellular structure slid into a human phase. No vampire power to keep him safe. Just himself and the gun strapped to his ribs. He'd gotten used to the sensation, but it never failed to make him nervous. He reminded himself that as soon as he managed to get out of the UV rays, he'd go back to being his bad-ass vampire self. But just in case, he had brought some muscle.

Bec and Sasha were also armed with weapons and their Lycan nature. It should be noted that even without going furry, they enjoyed more strength, stamina, and durability than humans. When it came to the perfect soldier twenty-four seven? Always go with Lycans. Pricey but loyal, which was their most valuable asset.

"Where to, boss?" Sasha asked, heading for the highway.

"Hospital."

"Looking for a snack?" Bec asked.

His guards thought themselves comedians. "I need to visit the maternity ward."

Bec and Sasha exchanged a glance, and Frederick sighed. "Not for food, you idiots. Someone's claiming I'm a daddy."

"You, a daddy?" That got more looks exchanged and then snickers.

"You both know my new condition makes it possible." He'd had to admit to his frailty the first time he had them stop to buy condoms.

Sasha took a hand off the steering to wave it. "Yeah, we know. But it's not like you're out banging everything in sight. Rumor has it your stash of rubbers is collecting dust."

Was nothing in his life private? "This happened more than nine months ago. The first time I went out."

"Oh. *Oooohhh*." It was the universal sound of understanding. Followed by more giggles.

His lips pursed as he glared at the backs of their heads. Platinum blonde for Bec, the sides shaved short but long and floppy on top. Sasha kept her dark curls close cropped as well.

"Care to share the amusement?" he grumbled.

"I mean, have you even thought of it? You and a baby? Can't see it." Bec snickered.

"Why not?" He couldn't have said why he argued when he didn't care. He'd already come to the conclusion he couldn't be the father.

"You're a vampire," Bec pointed out as if that said it all.

"I could be a parent if I wanted."

"Sure, you could, boss. You want to change diapers and deal with three a.m. feedings and screaming, then you do whatever turns your crank. So long as you're not eating any babies. I'll turn a blind eye to lots of stuff, but that crosses a line." Sasha made her boundaries clear.

He held in his next annoyed huff. "Have you ever known me to go near children?"

"Just making sure."

"It's a wonder I haven't eaten the disrespectful lot of you," he growled.

"Don't be grouchy. You know you love us, boss," Sasha declared.

"Like an annoying younger sibling who won't go away," he muttered but with no real heat.

He might insult them and drive them hard when needed, but those working under him, like the few he'd turned, were his family. It was why he never fucked any of them. But he'd been known to eat those who fucked with those he considered family.

Sasha dropped him and Bec at the hospital entrance. The maternity ward wasn't hard to find with all the signs in green and yellow leading the way.

Even better, there were no windows here, meaning he was himself and not a vulnerable human. Reaching his destination, it took only a few words of explanation, his name, and a bit of eye-to-eye contact to mesmerize a few people into shortening the whole prove-your-identity bullshit before he was ushered down a hall to a window. It looked upon a friendly room with a rocking chair in a corner.

Frederick waited alone. He'd left Bec at the nurses' station when they'd kicked up a fuss about a non-family member and obvious bodyguard following him. Since the pandemic, visitors had been strictly curtailed. It provided a defense of sorts for Frederick, especially since even his enemies would balk at attacking him here. It helped that no one expected him to be out and about at this time of day.

The door to the windowed room opened, and a nurse wheeling a bassinet entered. She rolled it to the viewing glass. The cold-hearted vampire who'd never wanted children, didn't actually like them, looked into that little face, and it hit him.

Hard.

*This is my child.*

The certainty buckled his knees, and he sagged against the glass. Put his hand on it and stared down at the perfect features of his sleeping heir.

He might have stood there forever if a soft female hadn't interrupted, asking, "Are you okay?"

Didn't she feel the world tilt? "I have a daughter."

## CHAPTER FOUR

THE GUY MANAGED to appear utterly blown away. The window held him up, and he looked unhealthily pale.

Klementine took a step back in case he went down. Last time she was nice to a guy barely holding himself together he puked all over the front of her shirt and groped her.

"Not sure why you're so surprised," she sassed. "Babies happen when grownups do the wild thing." Klementine's foster-mama taught her that at a young age. And Bernice would know. Five natural-born kids, three daddies, and still looking for Mr. Right. Mother Bernice, while almost forty years older than Klementine, was also technically her half-sister, which wasn't something spoken about, as people would question the math of it.

The almost fainting man glanced at her. Dark-haired, even darker gaze, handsome, too. He seemed familiar. Was he famous? An actor? The outer suburbs of New York had plenty.

"I swear it wasn't my fault."

"Is not a valid excuse if you stuck your you-know-what into her you-know-who." His shell-shocked expression was getting rather old.

"I thought I was sterile," he blurted out, and his eyes widened as if he'd said too much.

That explained his surprise. "Guess you were wrong." Klementine peeked down at the baby with her mess of blonde curls. Must take after her mom. She slept on her back, rosebud lips relaxed, slobber rolling off her chin. "She's cute."

"She is perfect," he declared.

"What's her name?"

He hesitated. "I don't know."

"Did her mom name her? What's the little card say?" As she bent down to peek at the name, she froze. For one, she knew the mother, Coralline Starfish. Klementine was on an emergency contact list. The hospital had called when she died.

*"We regret to inform you..."*

As Klementine listened, tears had rolled down her cheeks. Poor Coralline. A foster sister with a wild side who didn't deserve to die.

When she'd asked, *"Who shot her?"* the hospital had no answer other than, *"The police are looking into it."*

Who would want to kill Coralline?

And then the hospital went on to say, *"The baby survived."*

*"What baby?"* She'd almost passed out at the news and rushed over as fast as she could, which was still more than a few hours since she didn't live in the city.

The one thing Klementine didn't know was the name of the father. But she saw it now, clearly printed on the card inside the plastic sleeve for the bassinet.

She recognized the name, but she had to ask to be sure. "You're Frederick Thibodeaux?"

"Yes." He only spared her a quick glance, too fascinated by the baby.

*"The* Frederick Thibodeaux?" It couldn't be. It was too sunny outside.

"Depends. What have you heard about me?" he asked, giving her only part of his attention.

What hadn't she heard? A mobster whose

enemies had a tendency of backing down. The bodies never surfaced. People just disappeared. But what could you expect given his ingrained nature?

And here he was, staring down at Coralline's baby. Claiming it was his.

Like hell. "You are not the father."

He turned his full attention on her. "I am."

She shook her head. "It's impossible. You said it yourself. You're impotent."

His brows rose. "I said I thought I was sterile. I assure you nothing is wrong with my virility."

The emphasis on the word sent a shiver through her. "I don't care what you think or that card says. You can't be that child's father."

"And what makes you such a genetic expert?"

"Because you are a vampire."

CHAPTER FIVE

THE CLAIM HAD Frederick freezing before slowly turning to confront the woman. "A vampire?" he mocked.

How did this tiny human with her pixie-cut blonde hair and jewel-bright eyes know to accuse him? Only his enemies knew about his nature.

The realization had him staring intently at her. Inside, with no daylight to stifle, his power to mesmerize had him purring, "Who are you?

She blinked. "Klementine."

Like a succulent orange. Tasty. "Why are you here, Klementine?" He kept his voice low and hypnotic.

She replied slowly. "My friend had a baby."

"What friend?"

"Coralline."

The revelation startled. "Coralline was your friend?"

She took a slow moment to respond with a nod.

"What did she tell you about her pregnancy?"

"She didn't. I found out today when the hospital called."

"So you had no idea?"

Another head shake. "We used to be close when young, but as we got older, we went in different directions."

"Yet here you are."

"I'm here to handle her affairs and make arrangements for Anemone."

"Who?"

Her gaze went to the baby. "When we were kids, Coralline wanted to name her daughter after her grandma, Anemone."

"Like fuck is my child being named after a sea creature." Frederick turned from her, breaking their linked gaze.

"First off, I'm pretty sure she meant anemone the flower, and second, it's not up to you to decide."

He cast her a dark glance. "Actually, it is. My blood runs through her veins."

"The woman I spoke to said Coralline didn't want you to know."

"Then she shouldn't have put my name down as father."

He saw the moment Klementine decided to grasp at straws. "Just because Coralline said Anemone is yours doesn't mean it's true. Coralline was a free spirit."

"Did you just call your dead friend a whore? That's cold." He tsked and shook his head.

The woman's cheeks turned bright. "I did not. Just saying there's a possibility the baby isn't yours. She doesn't look anything like you."

"And yet she is most definitely related to me." He didn't need the official results to know that child was his, but the hospital required it.

"You can't have her," Klementine boldly declared.

"You don't get to have a say in this. I'm done with this conversation. Good day, Klementine." He extricated himself from that awkward conversation to insert himself into another with hospital administration. He demanded they hand his baby over.

Apparently, it wasn't that simple. The paperwork appeared interminable, but his lawyers handled it. While they waited for the results of the

DNA test, Frederick visited his daughter every day in the nursery where she thrived, and he learned more than he wanted about bottle feeding and diapers.

As if he'd be doing the menial work. In between visits with his baby and business, he interviewed nannies. He'd rejected a dozen so far, some highly vaunted humans he could mesmerize into being perfect servants. Even a few Lycans already in his employ who said they would teach the baby to fight the moment it learned to crawl and could latch onto an ankle. He even allowed a vampire of his line to apply. He turned them all down because none of them were right.

Given his many responsibilities, the nanny Frederick chose would be with his child more often than he would. He needed someone with strength to protect and wisdom to teach. But not someone cruel. He wouldn't have someone like his old tutor, always slapping for no reason.

The nanny, ideally, would know something of his world because living in close contact with Frederick would make it almost impossible for a nanny to ignore the strange comings and goings and the howling on full moons.

The nanny couldn't be annoying, as he'd have

to tolerate their presence. Female because he was sexist when it came to certain tasks.

Frederick was still hemming and hawing between the least horrible two options when he brought Anemone home.

Not the name she'd keep. Problem being he'd yet to find the right name for his daughter. It had to be just right.

He had all his bodyguards with him to escort her from the hospital. He would take no chances with his child. They split into three large SUVs, with Frederick and the baby riding in the middle one. His daughter slept in the car seat he'd strapped her into. The best on the market. He had a blanket tucked around her. Creamy cashmere. Soft for his daughter's precious skin.

When the truck accelerated, he snapped, "Watch it. Baby on board." Which reminded him, he should get those signs for the windows.

"Uh. Okay, boss," Sasha replied while Bec snickered.

Let them laugh. He knew his duty to this child.

Her tiny mouth opened and yawned.

So cute. Then so loud!

The noise that emerged from the tiny hole went from squeak to full-blown bellow in seconds.

"What's wrong with her?" he exclaimed. She'd never made this sound in the hospital. "Turn around. We need to take her back. She's broken."

"Annie's just crying, boss," Sasha declared. Having decided she hated the baby's name, she'd shortened it.

"Just? She is obviously in pain. Listen to her."

He stroked a finger on the baby's cheek, and she stopped mid scream and hiccupped. She nuzzled his finger and quieted.

"Ah, the baby likes the boss," Bec crooned.

"At least someone does," Sasha said on a snicker.

Let them jest. Obviously, his daughter knew he'd look after her.

A belief that sustained him until they got home and her fire-engine scream started again. But this time no amount of cheek strokes stopped it.

His perfect daughter had turned into a red-faced, screaming, fragile bundle of unhappiness who cried and shook her fists, and he had no idea what to do.

Which was when the woman from the hospital walked in. More like barged in.

"How did you get past my security?"

"I told them you hired me for sex."

He blinked. "And they believed you?"

"You saying I'm not hot enough to charge for it?" Klementine shot him an angry look before focusing on the baby. "Why haven't you taken her out of the car seat?"

"It keeps her safe."

"You idiot. Babies need to be held." She unclipped the harness and pulled out his daughter, tucked her close. "There, there, Anemone."

"That's not her name."

"Really? What is it then? Come on, dazzle me with your brilliant suggestion."

How did she know he'd yet to decide? He latched onto Sasha's shortened version. "Annie."

"Cute."

It was, actually. He scowled. "Why are you here?"

"To help you out by taking Annie off your hands."

## CHAPTER SIX

IF KLEMENTINE EXPECTED him to be grateful, she'd guessed wrong.

The man exploded, but quietly, the anger seething icily from him. "You are not taking my daughter anywhere."

His gaze bored into hers, and she felt him pushing at her, prodding at the barriers of her mind.

*Don't let him in.* If he knew the secrets tucked inside...she'd never leave his house alive.

Klementine bounced the quieting baby tucked against her shoulder, one hand cupped behind Anemone's head. "Stop glaring. You're obviously not handling the whole fatherhood thing well. My solution leaves your hands clean."

"You can't seriously expect me to hand my child over as if she's an object?" His tone hit impressive notes of incredulity. "That's my daughter."

"And? You're obviously not equipped to deal with her."

"What makes you think you are?"

"Coralline was my sister."

"I thought you said friend."

"Friend and sister."

He uttered a disdainful snort. "Neither makes you qualified."

"I had plenty of siblings I helped care for when I was living at home." Mother Bernice never had enough hands for all the kids she took in.

"If you're so gifted at caring for them, then have a baby of your own. This one is mine, and I can afford to hire professional help."

Her lips flattened. "Anemone should be raised by family." Raised by someone who would teach her about her mother, and her heritage. Something a vampire could never do.

"By your own claim, you're not blood related."

"Close enough. She was my foster sister, which is as strong a tie as any."

"I disagree that anyone willing to saddle a child with that name should be raising anyone."

How dare he argue? So what if he was the father? Monsters shouldn't be allowed to raise babies. Especially not a baby with a secret.

"I bet you can't even remember the color of Coralline's eyes." The baby deserved to be raised by someone who'd known her mother well. Who'd once loved her like a sister.

The smirk on his lips proved entirely too smug. "Aquamarine. Her hair was blonde. And she had a dimple."

Klementine scowled. "Maybe you remember what she looks like, but you don't know anything about her."

"And? Plenty of children only ever know one parent. I'm sure I can create a proper martyr for my daughter to look up to."

She gaped. "You'd lie?"

"Don't act so shocked. What else could I do? You seem to forget your friend is hardly innocent. She never sought me out once to inform me. Would have hidden it from me quite possibly had she not been in that accident."

"Being shot is not an accident."

"Perhaps. But it doesn't change the facts. Would she have told me if not for that fatal wound?"

"I don't know." Klementine's shoulders slumped. "No one knew. Not even Mother Bernice." And that hurt. At one time, they'd shared everything. How could they have grown so far apart? Now it was too late. She couldn't ask for another chance with her sister, which was why she had to earn her forgiveness doing right by the baby.

"My daughter has other family?" He sounded almost surprised.

"Yes and no. Her bio mom gave her up." She didn't add hers did the same. "Bernice was our foster mom." Who put up with a lot when Coralline hit her teens and began running away. When Coralline reached adulthood, she left and never came back, only barely keeping in touch with Klementine. It had been more than a year since they'd last talked, still, once sisters, always sisters, especially given their shared secrets.

"Since Bernice isn't a blood relative, and never adopted Coralline, she has no claim." He stated it as if he suddenly worried Bernice might try and steal the baby. Only if she thought she'd get some extra bucks.

"You really intend to keep her?" She couldn't help a note of incredulity. "To do what?"

"Raise her as I see fit."

"She should be raised by someone who knew her mom."

"You're welcome to visit."

She made a last-ditch effort. "Anemone is the only living link left of Coralline."

"Then you'll be relieved to know she will be raised in luxury."

"Without a mom."

"Who says I'm not married?" He arched a brow.

"I looked you up. You're single." If often pictured with gorgeous women. Thibodeaux had an active nightlife. Vampires often did. Only, he didn't fit the profile, given he stood in a room flooded with daylight.

Was the information about him wrong?

"My daughter won't lack for female role models," he declared. "And I would remind you, Coralline had no issue with raising my child without a father. Now if you don't mind, hand over my daughter."

It was with reluctance Klementine peeled the baby from her shoulder. She couldn't exactly keep her, even if she wanted to take the baby and run. Thibodeaux as the father had all the legal rights.

Bernice wouldn't care about Coralline's baby. That left only Klementine in Anemone's corner. The only thing standing between an innocent life and a murderous vampire. Because, after leaving the hospital, she'd double-checked with her sources. They all agreed he was a creature of darkness. A drinker of blood and not someone to screw with.

She had her doubts, though. And even if she didn't, she couldn't walk away.

"Have you hired a nanny?" she asked as she handed the calmed baby over to him.

Thibodeaux handled Anemone like a fragile egg, barely moving as he brought her to his chest. The softness that creased his features hit Klementine hard.

*He really cares.*

So what if he looked happy with the baby tucked close? Could be he imagined Anemone as his next meal. She didn't actually believe it, though.

"Who knew choosing a nanny would be so fraught with annoyance."

"Are you having problems finding one?" she asked.

"I'm interviewing several at the moment."

"You need to hire one, ASAP."

He shrugged. "I will when I find one good enough for my daughter."

She ignored the cuteness of his statement and sprang on the opening he created. "I can be the nanny."

He laughed. "You're not mentally stable enough for the job."

That brought a grimace to her lips. "I am not crazy. I'd take good care of her."

He shook his head. "It won't work. You're too emotionally involved."

"Doesn't that make me a better choice? I'll love her like she's my own."

"Given my business hours, I need someone living on the premises."

"That's not a problem. I can move in." Her apartment could sit vacant for the days or weeks it took to convince Thibodeaux to hand over Anemone or figure out how to steal her before the child came to harm.

"This is a full-time job, you realize. If you don't do it well, I will fire you."

"And if you're a shitty father, I'll have her removed from your care." Klementine would protect her from Thibodeaux and find out why this supposed vampire wasn't acting as he should.

He arched a brow. "Is your plan to try and trick me into losing her?"

"I would never lie. But I will make sure she's safe." She kept her chin high. Being awfully bold in the face of handsome evil.

For some reason, this drew a bark of laughter, which startled the baby. Her eyes flew open. Brilliant jewels of blue with a hint of green, just like Coralline's. For a second, her mouth worked, and her body squirmed.

The man holding her froze. Didn't even breathe until the baby settled on his shoulder again.

Thibodeaux caught Klementine watching him. "How about a trial run? You prove you're decent at the job and you can stay. But if you are to be a live-in nanny, then you must understand there are rules you'll have to follow."

"What kind of rules?"

"Basic ones, such as signing a nondisclosure

about anything you see or hear. No visitors on the property. No images posted to social media."

"Paranoid much?"

"Yes." Spoken flatly. "Given my stature in society, I have enemies."

"Which explains all the guards. Afraid one of the people you've screwed will come after you?"

"In business, there are losers, and some don't handle it with grace. The weak ones would retaliate for my success. My guards are there to prevent anything from happening, so you'll stay inside at night to avoid incident and, in the daytime, notify security if you're taking a walk on the grounds."

"Would you like me to wear a signal collar so you can track me?"

"No need. We have an app that loads on your phone. Which will be with you at all times."

"Going to spy on me?"

"Yes." He didn't even pretend.

"Sounds kind of illegal and invasive."

"As I said before, I have enemies, which means I don't take chances. Don't like it, then don't take the nanny job."

"Will you be bugging my room and phone calls, too?"

"Would you like me to?"

Her lips pursed. "No. Of course not." Only to offer him a cocky smile as she added, "Unless you like to watch."

His nostrils flared. The only sign, and yet it let her know he didn't entirely tell the truth when he said, "I'm more a man of action."

Did he have voyeuristic tendencies?

Why did she even care?

"I'm boring to watch, FYI," she felt a need to mention.

"I highly doubt that," he muttered. "When can you start?"

"Now."

"Don't you need to go get your stuff?"

"Anemone is probably getting close to a feeding, so I'll wait until she's done, and then we can go for a ride."

"No," he barked. "I don't want her leaving this property."

Klementine thought about pushing it, but she didn't need him kicking her out so quickly. "Fine. In that case I'll have one of my sisters drop off my stuff. I assume you have a room to give me, with its own bathroom, close to the baby?"

"Aren't you going to ask how much it pays first?"

Her lips tilted as she teased, "Pay me what you think your daughter's care is worth."

"Well played." A smile ghosted his lips. "You'll give me a list of supplies needed for the baby."

"What do you have so far?" she asked.

"I'm not sure. I had my staff throw together a nursery."

"Let's see what it's got."

He led the way, still holding the baby awkwardly as if she would leap from his arms to her death at any second. The anxiety in his posture made it hard to remember her automatic dislike.

Was Thibodeaux not the man she'd been told about? The rumors she'd heard had him as a cold killer. A monster of the night who drank blood and let no one get in his way.

As he passed windows with streaming light, she had to wonder. Vampires couldn't do daylight.

It killed them. Set them on fire. Vampires didn't stand in a puddle of it for a second and lightly say, "Beautiful day."

Thibodeaux led them to the second floor, down a hall that ended in double doors. But her door was closer to the stairs. Oversized paneling with an intricate doorknob led into a lovely suite. The bedroom, done in tones of cream, gold, and pale pink, was massive, with an ensuite that included a jet tub and a large, multi-head walk-in shower. There was a closet bigger than her apartment bedroom. A fireplace. Even a coffee maker and mini bar with drinks and snacks. No alcohol she noticed.

The door to the nursery had a security panel that required a passcode or handprint.

"Worried someone will kidnap her?"

"Yes." He didn't sound as if he joked.

"Like who?" She half expected him to blame her.

Only he shrugged. "A man in my position has enemies and has to take precautions."

Did he suspect one of his enemies was in his midst?

Thibodeaux activated the unit by pressing his hand on the screen, before saying, "Add authorized user. Security level, domestic staff." He glanced at her. "Say your name."

"Klementine."

He stepped aside. "Put your hand on the panel so it can scan you."

She didn't like the idea of having her print on file, but she didn't have much choice. She placed her hand on it, and it flashed a few times before going dark.

"All set up. So long as you have a pulse and don't show heightened anxiety, the door will open at your touch or if you ask it to."

"Hold on, so if someone breaks into this house, takes me hostage, and tries to force me to open that door, it will fail if I'm freaking out?"

"Yes."

"Damn. That is some impressive security."

"It's a converted panic room."

"Worried about attack?"

"It's doubtful anyone would get that far."

"Let's take a peek at your baby fortress," she muttered as she once more touched the screen. This time when it illuminated, and the door clicked, she opened it.

She entered a windowless space that lit softly the moment she crossed the threshold. Tiny lights ringed the room.

"Brighter," he demanded, and the room lightened, showing it was of a similar cream-colored design with hints of yellow and mauve.

A crib, intricately carved and solid, took place of pride in the center. It was lined with creamy soft linen. Over it hung a mobile of fantastical creatures that included a gryphon and a unicorn.

A gorgeous nursery and not what she'd have expected. Fredericklay the baby in the bed and stepped back.

Thibodeaux stood staring by the rail for a moment before murmuring, "Don't make me regret hiring you, Klementine."

"Going to kill me and bury me under your roses if I piss you off?"

"I wouldn't let you off that easy," was his purred threat as he left.

She took a moment before she followed, emerging into her temporary bedroom to see he'd closed the hall door after himself.

She was alone. Maybe.

She glanced around, seeking the camera. She wondered if he was watching her. Listening. Let him.

He'd soon see he had nothing to fear. He could trust her. Relax. And when he did…then she'd take Anemone far away from here.

## CHAPTER SEVEN

WITH LONG STRIDES, Frederick returned to his office. He tried to concentrate on the business requiring his attention. But how could he with the baby and his new nanny occupying his mind?

His daughter was home, and he'd never been more aware of the danger that surrounded him. It wasn't that long ago the Fae had moved against him, attacking his property with their mercenary allies of goblins and trolls. They wanted to kill him simply for existing. In their mind, vampires were an abomination, especially one not impressed by their supposed Fae court.

They'd been sparring for centuries, ever since

he rejected one of the Fae's upper-echelon ladies. Although lady was a stretch.

Apparently, rejection didn't suit her. She'd carried a vendetta since. Had been raising the bounty on his head for years. Even targeted his staff.

What would his enemy do to a child of his loins?

Especially a child who might not be fully human.

Now if only they could figure out what his daughter was. Anthony had been hard at work, deciphering what Annie's unexpected DNA meant. As expected, the strand had some variances. Some directly related to Frederick. But others...Anthony claimed he'd never seen the like.

But Frederick had an idea of what it meant.

Of what Coralline might have been.

If his theory was correct, then it would be doubly, triply important to keep his daughter's presence a secret. He couldn't let anyone get their hands on her.

The fear of it led to him calling Lexie. "I need your help."

Lexie refused. "Can't. I'm already too busy."

"But it's important. And it's not for me, but my daughter."

The statement brought a heavy sigh from her. "I still can't help, but I do have a friend I can recommend."

The friend, Callum Perth, arrived within the hour, big, burly, and—given the hair and the smell —all bear. Rare this side of the border. Canadians didn't tend to migrate.

At Callum's arrival, Frederick didn't rise from behind his desk but did indicate a chair. "Thank you for coming on short notice. Lexie says you're good at digging up information."

"Yup."

A man of few words. Frederick had no problem with that so long as he was good at his job. "Here's what I need you to do." He handed over the picture he'd printed of Klementine, who'd filled in the bogus online employee form the moment Sasha brought it to her room.

Klementine Sunflower had an apartment on the other side of town in a converted warehouse. She worked at a bagel shop of all things and hadn't yet quit, given her boss expected her to show up for her shift the next day.

She had a credit card balance of one hundred

and seventy-three dollars. Her bank account held just over two hundred. No pets. No car. She took the bus or relied on ride sharing to get places.

As Frederick handed over the file, he explained. "Klementine is my daughter's live-in nanny. She was close friends with my child's mother." He passed over the little he'd gleaned of Coralline Starfish. No known address. Or job. Nothing but a picture obtained from the morgue and an autopsy report. No fluids or samples because she'd been cremated only hours after her death on Klementine's orders.

Lastly, he pulled up a video of his sleeping daughter. His very perfect and precious daughter.

"It is important we find out who Klementine is and who she might be working for. I won't have my child hurt."

"What's the baby's name?"

He almost gnashed his teeth as he had to admit, "She doesn't have one yet."

"Ah. I see."

"See what?"

"People only name things they're planning to keep." The most Callum had said, and it irritated him.

"On the contrary, I am going through this

trouble to ensure she has the longest life. Be warned, anyone who harms a hair on her head, or abets in such harm, will end up flayed alive."

"Got it." Then the grudging bear added, "She's cute."

"I know." Frederick now understood why fathers became overprotective of their daughters.

When Callum left, Frederick turned the monitors back on. It took a while to locate the new nanny, strutting around his chateaux, baby strapped to her chest, poking in corners she shouldn't.

Which was why it was so much fun to suddenly pop out and say, "Looking for something?"

## CHAPTER EIGHT

THE MAN TOOK stealthy to the next level. One minute, Klementine was attempting to find out more about Thibodeaux, and the next, he was whispering in her ear and she whirled to strike.

He caught her fist mid-swing and arched a brow. "Good to know you're ready to defend yourself."

"Why are you sneaking up on me?" she hissed.

"Hardly sneaking since this is my house. You seemed rather intent. What did you find so interesting?"

Her gaze went to the painting on the wall. Framed in gilded wood, it showed an austere couple and a young boy. It appeared quite old.

"Family portrait?" she asked.

"My ancestors. Long dead. Until recently, I was last of my line."

He lied. She knew it was him in the painting. The resemblance was too striking, yet he persisted in pretending. "You don't have an heir. Anemone has her mother's last name."

"No, she doesn't. When I eventually file for her birth certificate it will be with my name."

"Too late."

"Excuse me?"

"When I was handling Coralline's affairs at the hospital I was asked to sign off on some paperwork. The registration of Anemone's birth was part of it." She probably shouldn't have sounded so pleased with herself.

His expression darkened. "You did what?"

"I wasn't going to have her nameless or have Coralline's dying wish ignored."

"What dying wish? You admitted you'd not seen her in a while."

"She's still family, and I know what she wanted."

"You had no legal right, and you know it. Which means you committed fraud."

"When did she get teeth?" he mused aloud, reaching for her, and grateful for some help getting her out of the sling.

"Shouldn't you be finding out what happened to your window?" she asked even as she aided him in transferring the baby, who nuzzled close.

"I know what happened," was his ominous reply a second before Norris, one of his day guards, strode in and turned pale at the sight of them standing amidst broken glass.

"Oh shit," Norris muttered.

He should sound nervous. Frederick leaned over and plucked the baseball from the shards.

"I take it this belongs to you?"

Norris swallowed and nodded rather than speak.

Had it just been the two of them, Frederick might have shoved the ball where the sun would never shine, even if a week ago, he wouldn't have cared about a broken window. That was before his daughter. Before she'd almost gotten injured.

He handed Norris the ball and said softly, "Annie could have been hurt. Move the games away from the house."

No other rebuke and yet Norris slunk out of

there, proverbial tail between the legs. He'd work four times as hard now to prove his worth.

Klementine said nothing until they were alone. "I think you just scared the piss out of him."

"He acted irresponsibly."

"And rather than punish him, you were icy. Your disappointment thick enough it wouldn't crack. Impressive."

He cast her a glance. "You find this amusing?"

"I do, especially since he's a werewolf and they're not easy to intimidate."

"Such a vivid imagination. First vampires. Now werewolves. What's next? Dragons?"

"Everyone knows they're extinct."

Did they? He'd never heard it spoken in the absolute before.

"I hate to break it to you, but dragons and vampires don't exist."

"I don't know why you'd bother to lie. It's obvious to anyone paying attention."

"With statements like that, I have to wonder at my choice in hiring you." Wondered how she knew. Did she have to die? His secret wasn't one he shared easily.

She stepped forward, and when her hand lifted, he expected either a slap or a caress. Instead, she plucked glass from his shoulder and held it up. "You'll ruin your reputation as a blood thirsty monster if you keep acting like a hero."

Then she walked off.

Leaving him stunned and with grudging respect. Not many had the balls to stand up to him. Even fewer left him speechless.

Soon after, he made his way to his office, knowing his staff would handle the damage. Watching her on the camera, feeding the baby and playing with her, he only barely heard the knock at his door.

"Come in."

Callum entered and said, "Bars."

"What?"

"On windows. Prevents missiles."

Sound advice but he was feeling contrary. "Or I could order the staff to play away from the chateaux."

"Bars and drones," Callum insisted.

"No machines. For eyes in the sky, I prefer ravens." He kept a trained flocked to handle possible avian intruders. The Fae had been known to try and send sprites, even a gnome once or twice. Although the second time could have just been a joke. After all, just because they found a small shoe in the cat's bed didn't mean it ate one.

"I met your baby mama on the way in."

"She's not the baby's mama," he growled.

"Don't be so sure." Callum suddenly strung more than three words together. "I tracked down the birth registration she tried to file. She put herself as the mother, father unknown."

He almost lost his shit. "Why that conniving... brilliant woman. I can't believe she tried that." A good thing Callum snared it before it became permanent. "You got rid of it?"

"Yes. All traces of the baby's birth have been erased."

"Good. What about the nurses working that night?"

"Without records, they've got no proof even if someone came around asking."

It helped Frederick had altered their memories slightly, making them believe his name was Derrick Theabough.

All links leading to him had been taken care of except for Klementine. As if it were a trigger, Julian buzzed him.

"What is it, Julian?" he asked.

"Um, your nanny wants to see you."

He straightened and refrained from immediately barking to let her in. Couldn't look too eager.

"It better be important," he grumbled, knowing she was listening.

The office door opened, and she strode in, only to halt upon seeing Callum. "You're busy."

"Yes and no. You might want to hear what my man, Callum, has to say. He's been looking into your friend's murder," he said bluntly to harden himself against how much he liked seeing her walk in, his baby nestled to her chest.

"You know something about Coralline's death?" She swayed and blanched.

He felt like an ass in that moment for springing that on her, but in his defense, she kept throwing him off balance. He had to do something to counter her allure. "Tell us what you've found out."

Callum tucked his hand behind his back and provided a succinct report. "Police are still calling Coralline's death a random act of violence. Wrong place. Wrong time."

"But?" Frederick prompted.

"Screams targeted to me," Callum said with a shrug.

"What? You're wrong," Klementine exclaimed. "Why would anyone want to kill Coralline?"

"No motive yet," Callum reported.

Frederick provided a lengthier explanation. "The cops are convinced it's random. But I'm less inclined to think so. It would seem Coralline has been hiding for at least the last few months. It took some digging to find her current address. She was paying for her apartment in cash and using an assumed name."

"Sounds like she was scared. Of you, maybe?" Klementine offered him a lasered accusation.

He laughed. "Why would I want to kill her?"

"Because maybe you lied. Maybe she did tell you about the pregnancy and you snapped."

He arched a brow. "You really think me that cold? If that were true, what would I be capable of right now do you think?"

She obviously realized she'd gone too far and struggled to hide her fear. "If you kill me, people will know and come looking."

"I'll have an alibi and plenty of witnesses to your mauling by wild animals."

"You're threatening me?" she squeaked.

"More like proving how inane you sound. I didn't kill your friend. But someone did."

"Do you think Anemone is in danger?" She

chewed her lower lip. "Coralline's dead. Why would they come after a baby?"

He'd seen evil in his time. "I'm thinking we'll need to add more security."

"What she needs is a different home." Klementine's solution.

"This is her home."

"It's sad you're talking about making it a fortress and don't see a problem with that."

The rebuke brought a frown. "Was there a reason for your visit?"

"I'm going to put her down for a nap and then run across town and get my stuff."

He noticed a glint of glass in her hair.

"Don't move." He plucked it, only to see another caught in the strands. "You have shards in your hair."

"Oh shoot. The baby." She leaned away from the child.

"I'll take her," Frederick declared.

"Aren't you covered, too?" she pointed out.

"I'll take the baby." Callum's blunt fingers reached for Annie.

They might have protested had the man not shown how adept he was at not only extricating the baby but flopping her onto his shoulder while not once waking her up. Perhaps he'd hired the wrong nanny.

"I've got the baby. Go get your stuff." The man strode off, and Klementine had to ask, "Are you sure he can be trusted?"

"More than you since he comes with impeccable references."

"I wouldn't hurt Anemone."

"My daughter no, but you don't like me."

She bit her lip. "I never said that."

"Maybe not but you've done a poor job of hiding it. I know what you did on the birth certificate. Putting yourself down as mother. Major fraud, as in get-your-ass- thrown-in-jail kind of illegal."

"I did that just in case things didn't work out with you. I've been in foster care."

"I won't abandon my daughter. And yet you persist in thinking the worst of me. Why?"

"I don't think the worst of you," she badly lied.

"Is this because you still think I'm a vampire?"

She hesitated before saying, "Are you going to deny you're a mobster?"

"I prefer to call myself a man of business."

She uttered a snort. "Whatever floats your boat."

"Shall we go outside?"

"Why?"

"One, so you can see I won't burn to a crisp, and two, because I have a vacuum in the garage to rid us of the glass."

"I should shower and change."

"After. You wouldn't want to cut yourself while bathing."

He grabbed her by the arm and led her quickly down the back steps, knowing the fastest route. Once in the massive garage, she stopped balking and stared in open-mouthed astonishment.

"It's a parking lot." She referenced the neat rows of vehicles.

"I like variety."

"You have six Suburbans."

"Fantastic trucks."

"And eight motorcycles."

"I hate riding alone."

She shook her head. "You are the height of male arrogance and privilege."

"I don't see why I should hide my wealth. Isn't my consumption a good thing for the economy?"

She laughed. "You have an answer for everything."

And she wasn't the least bit daunted by him. Nor flirtatious.

It left Frederick intrigued. He didn't run into many women who weren't impressed by him. Between his money and power, women constantly threw themselves at him.

The station for detailing his cars had a powerful vacuum system setup that roared when activated. It also sucked her hair into the tube, which had her squealing and laughing. A laughter that trebled when she snatched it from him and suctioned his hair into spikes.

He must have looked ridiculous, and yet he didn't bat at her hands or ask her what the fuck she was doing. He joined her in laughter, and when they wrestled for the hose, it seemed only natural she ended up in his arms.

Looking up at him.

Both of them suddenly still and silent.

She broke it by saying, "I should check on the baby."

A good thing she left because, for a moment, he'd almost forgotten about his rule about not kissing his staff.

## CHAPTER TEN

FREDERICK HAD ALMOST KISSED HER.

And she would have kissed him back. A realization that led to Klementine refusing his invitation to join him for dinner on the veranda, an intimate meal with a man who made her almost forget the crimes he was accused of.

Being somewhat sadistic and curious, she did peek outside and saw him sitting in the sun's setting rays, enjoying what looked to be a multi-course meal with wine. Probably the same stuffed chicken served to her in her room. His staff delivered it before she'd even thought of eating. While she was putting the baby to bed in the nursery, they cleared it away.

After a quick run across the city to pack a bag, she remained in her room that evening, watching television, nodding off in a chair until the monitor started hiccupping as the baby woke. Immediately, she moved. The bottle warmer she'd put on a list had been delivered and set up, the cans of high-end formula stored in a cupboard, a basket left for her to place the dirty discards. His staff were incredibly intuitive.

She grabbed a bottle, flipped it into the heater, and flew into the baby's room, only to find a shirtless daddy already standing there. She'd wondered where the locked door across from hers led to. Had an inkling, now confirmed.

Frederick reached for Anemone and tucked her to his bare chest, hushing, "Shh. Don't cry. I'm here."

And for a second that was enough. Anemone snuggled into her father and calmed to a shuddering, final sob. It was super cute. It didn't last, as baby's tummy made her grumpy.

Anemone wailed, and as if he'd known Klementine was there the entire time, Frederick's gaze flew to meet hers. "What's wrong with her?"

"She's hungry. At this age they eat every two hours or so."

"That often!" His brows rose super high. "Aren't you feeding her enough?"

"Babies have tiny bellies that aren't used to eating, plus these first few weeks babies usually double in size, meaning they're ravenous."

He eyed the top of his sobbing daughter's fluffy head. "Bigger might make her sturdier. She's fragile."

"She'll be like that for a while." Klementine tilted her head. "Bring her to my room. I've got a bottle ready."

She didn't check to see if he followed, just padded to the next room, and sure enough, the light on the warmer was green. She pulled the bottle free and tapped it on her inner forearm to test it.

"Good to go. Want to feed her?" she asked as she turned around to find him standing there, holding the wailing baby, looking ill at ease but not angry or violent.

"You want me to do it?" Again, so surprised.

"Yes, you. You are the daddy. You are supposed to feed her."

"I don't have milk."

"Idiot. It's not like you need to whip out a tit and shove it into her mouth. She's thirsty." She held out the bottle. "Just pop the nipple in her mouth. I've already pushed all the air out."

"Shouldn't I be sitting?" He truly looked afraid he'd drop her, and yet she'd bet he never dropped a damned thing. The man moved sinuously.

"If you want to sit, then sit. Cradle her like a football."

"I don't play sports."

"Maybe you should. Sit. Lighten up." She shoved him into the rocker with its thick seat and back cushion. He controlled his descent and sat stiffly, the baby still against his shoulder, yelling, her fists flailing.

He eyed her. "Now what?"

"Crook of your arm." Klementine showed him how to hold the baby, and he shifted her.

The moment Anemone hit her back, Klementine popped the nipple into her mouth. The yodeling stopped.

The relief on his face proved instant. "The bottle is a mute button for babies."

Her lips quirked. "It is. So, a good thing you're learning to do it. Although I'm surprised the hospital didn't show you."

He grimaced. "I made them show Sasha. I

couldn't handle those little rooms and the smell for long."

Or was it the temptation because he could smell the blood?

"What else do I do?" he asked, holding the bottle steady.

"Don't move."

"How will I know she's done?"

"She'll fall asleep."

The man held the bottle and watched the baby as if he'd never seen anything more wonderful. She certainly hadn't.

It made her wonder about her suspicions. Perhaps the rumors she'd heard about Thibodeaux were mistaken. According to the stories she knew, vampires didn't love. Or have children. They were monsters. She'd been told so by everyone who spoke of them growing up. But being taught something didn't make it the truth.

Still, over the next few days, as she cared for Anemone and got to see Frederick around her, she found herself intrigued by the man. Softened as she enjoyed the love he had for his child. Heated given how good he looked wearing only silky pajama bottoms and nothing else.

She had just about convinced herself that maybe, just maybe, she didn't have to act, when she caught him doing the most heinous thing.

CHAPTER ELEVEN

"ARE you licking the middle of the Oreos and throwing out the cookie?" Klementine demanded as she entered the kitchen in search of a snack a week after her arrival. A week that hadn't led to a single untoward thing happening, if she ignored the unusual amount of howling at night. Stupid country living.

Frederick stood in a pool of sunlight by the sink and froze, guilt written all over his face. "It's the best part," was his sheepish admission.

She wrinkled her nose. "Hell no, it isn't. Everyone knows it's all about the crunch of the cookie. Personally, I prefer mine with no cream." She snatched the top of the cookie from his hand, leaving him with the other half still thick with icing.

She popped it into her mouth and chewed.

He licked the cream from his and offered the other half with a twinkle in his eye. "Want it?"

"Heck yeah." She ate it, too.

"Share another?" He pointed to the box, and they might have eaten the whole thing if he hadn't suddenly grabbed her and dragged her to the floor. Before she could ask him what the fuck, glass shattered, and she gaped at the tile as she heard the crack of several gunshots.

That wasn't a baseball this time. Nor an accident.

"Don't move," he admonished softly, even as he ignored his own advice. He rolled and rose in one fluid motion, and despite his command, she shifted to a sitting position, wincing as her hand was pricked by a shard of glass.

Through her heavy breaths she heard snarling and yips. Someone had set dogs loose. Probably the same ones she heard at night. Odd, though, how she'd never seen any canines around. It only served to reinforce her belief that his staff were shapeshifters.

Glancing at Frederick, who stood to the side of

the window in shadows, she caught a glimpse of his stark features, the hint of fangs. Or was she mistaken? Because as he shifted into the sunlight, he appeared completely normal, if pissed.

"You're making yourself a target!" she hissed, not daring to stand quite yet.

"It's safe now." He sounded annoyed by the very concept. "My people are hunting down the perpetrator."

"Going to perform a citizen's arrest?"

Rather than reply, he glanced down at her and held out his hand. "Are you injured?"

"No." Once more, he'd protected her with his body. She'd not expected that, especially since she didn't have the baby on her this time. "Why was someone shooting at you?"

"Why assume it was for me?"

"Your castle. Seems kind of obvious."

"Do I look like the kind of man who hangs out in the kitchen? More likely my cook has made an enemy. Chefs are very competitive you know. And ours is a ladies' man."

Klementine pursed her lips. "You're being facetious."

"Fine. It was probably directed toward me. It happens. I'll handle it."

"Handle it how?"

"Do you really want to be an accessory to a crime?"

She blinked at him. "You're going to kill them?"

"That was a sniper. What would you suggest I do instead?"

"Call the cops."

She deserved his laughter.

"You going to solve two problems and have him for dinner?" she snapped.

"Ah, I see you still believe the rumors of me being a vampire."

"I don't know what you are," she said on a sigh. Nothing she'd seen of him seemed to fit the vampire mold. No blood sucking, no bats. Today was the first time she'd seen actual violence. For a mobster, he led a pretty boring life.

"Can't I just be a man?"

She stared at him. "We both know you're more than that."

She accidentally fed his arrogance. She saw it in the shift of his posture. She expected the slow, sensual smirk.

The surprise came from his next words. He

leaned in close to whisper, "You are right. I am a vampire. The monster you've been warned about."

She held her breath more in anticipation than fear. "Why are you telling me this?" Why now?

"Because I finally figured out what you are, Klementine. I can't believe I didn't sense it before. You're Fae."

## CHAPTER TWELVE

THE SECRET SPILLED into the open. A secret Klementine had done her best to not even think lest he read her mind. Could he read her mind? The stories had been wrong about so many things thus far. Such as the fact vampires were cold, heartless creatures.

She blinked at Frederick. "Excuse me?" She really hoped he didn't notice the stutter in her heart. Who was she kidding? He could probably smell her blood type.

"Drop the charade. I know you're Fae."

For a second longer, she debated lying before shrugging and saying. "Only half." Which might as well have been none according to her full-blood relatives. Snobbery thrived in her lineage.

"Half explains why your ears are round and you don't smell like them." He sounded quite annoyed. "Although I should have known by the ridiculous name."

"My name is not ridiculous."

"Really? Let me ask you, when you have children, are you going to name them after fruit? Maybe Pomegranate. Or will you stick to citrus like Orange or Grapefruit?"

"I'm not... That is... It's spelled with a K." A weak excuse. While full Fae had lovely, fanciful names, those mixed with human got relegated to animals, plants, and flowers.

"You didn't answer the question. When you have a child, are you going to saddle them with something ridiculous?"

"Because Frederick is so much better," she huffed, rolling her eyes. No way was she admitting she spent a good decade when younger with her heart set on naming her first daughter Portulaca.

He arched a brow. "You have a problem with a time-honored name?"

"I do. Frederick is boring and very unsexy. Wasn't

Freddy the name of a frog? Or was it a horse? I don't think there's too many heroes going by the name of Fred-er-ick." She teased the consonants of his name.

For some reason, this curved his lips. "A good thing I'm no hero."

He certainly wasn't, and she'd do well to remember that. "No kidding. Vampire." she said with a sneer she'd been taught, only to feel guilty. Would she really judge him based on what others said or what she'd seen thus far of the man himself?

Which admittedly wasn't much other than the fact he truly loved his daughter and his staff were extremely loyal.

"Better a vampire than a duplicitous and murderous Fae."

"We are not murderers!"

"Really? You should tell that to the assassins I deal with on an almost monthly basis. Like today." He eyed the broken window before grabbing her by the arm and leading her out of the pile of glass.

"What makes you think—"

He cut her off. "I am not arguing with you. The fact of the matter is the Fae have hated me for decades. It's what I get for refusing to bed one."

"The Fae don't hate you because you didn't

beguile one of them but because you drink their blood."

"Not often. It's a little too sweet for my taste."

Her jaw dropped. She couldn't tell if he was joking or not. "You just admitted to killing us."

He snorted. "No vampire enjoys drinking from a corpse. Nor are we so careless."

"Are you trying to convince me you're a responsible blood drinker?"

"Friends don't let friends get blood drunk," he said soberly, making their conversation even odder.

"Now that I know, what are you going to do?"

"You tell me. After all, I've apparently invited a Fae into my house. Are you a spy for them? An assassin?"

Her mouth rounded. "I'm not anything." She didn't admit the Fae wanted nothing to do with her.

"So you say and yet here you are."

"I'm here because I am one of the closest things Anemone has to family."

"And Fae stick together. When were you going to tell me Coralline wasn't fully human? It took Anthony a while to figure it out."

"Who's Anthony?"

"Don't change the subject. You still haven't

told me what I should do with a Fae spy." He led her into his office full of sunlight from the patio doors. The desk sat in the midst of it, and only there did he finally stop moving.

He glanced down at her. She didn't flinch when he brought up his hand and stroked a stray strand of hair.

"I should get changed. I'm probably covered in glass."

"That would be me, actually." He then proceeded to tear the buttons on his shirt and remove it, revealing a broad chest with a thin line of hair going down.

She swallowed. "I should check on the baby."

"Annie is fine. My phone hasn't buzzed." He lay the shirt on the desk. "Still waiting for your reply."

"I'm not a spy. And let me add, if you're going to judge me simply on the basis of my birth, then I should remind you that your daughter is also Fae."

"A quarter, which is barely." He waved a hand.

"What I don't understand is how you have a daughter." She forged ahead with the question because when she had tried to tell someone, they insisted it was impossible. Mocked her for it.

"Do I really need to explain how babies are

made? I could give you a demonstration," he purred and, with that deadly bared chest, eased into her space.

Too close. She could smell his cologne. The musk of him. He didn't reek of death or blood as expected, but man.

"Don't be crass." She fought his allure.

His laughter boomed. "Then don't ask stupid questions."

"Vampires can't make babies." It was physically impossible.

"You're right; they can't."

"And you're a vampire."

"I am."

"Then how?"

"So many questions, and yet I've yet to ask any of my own."

"Like what?"

"What would you do if I kissed you?"

CHAPTER THIRTEEN

FREDERICK COULDN'T HAVE SAID why he asked. It should have never left his mouth. He had more important things to do like find out if his people had caught the sniper and questioned them. Maybe multitask and turn the shooter into a snack.

Instead he'd asked to kiss her, and now the query hung out there, a reminder to them both of the previous embrace. Of the passion simmering under the surface.

"What makes you think I'm interested?" A huffy query.

"Because I know you feel it. This thing between us." He admitted it aloud and hoped she didn't mock him. When was the last time he'd felt such trepidation revealing an emotion? He didn't like it one bit.

It didn't help when she said, "I don't know what you're talking about." She tossed her head.

It might have annoyed him more if he hadn't sensed the lie. He shifted closer. "For me, when you're around, the air fills with electricity. Possibility. Awareness." He whispered the last a mere inch from her lips.

Her gaze held his. "It's just lust."

"If it's just lust, then why not assuage it?"

She licked her lips. "We really shouldn't. You're technically my boss."

"You're fired."

"I'm not leaving the baby."

"Then I guess we are at an impasse because I really want to kiss you." The honest, raw truth.

They stared at each other, a silent exchange that led to their lips meeting. He couldn't have said who moved first. He just knew he was kissing her, and she kissed him back, her mouth hungry on his. Ravenous.

He felt every hot lick, nip, and exhalation. In that moment, he was simply a man, and she a woman. The attraction between them real and wild.

He lifted her so that she sat on his desk, leaving him in a pool of sunlight that made him all too human. He pressed his body against her legs. Her knees parted, and he moved close. He reached for her ass to tuck her even more intimately, and her legs wrapped around him. Her arms twined, and her fingers clutched.

Off-the-charts passion.

It made him tremble. It made him ache. He wanted her badly. Now.

She proved just as frantic, nipping him in her excitement. She was the one to grab at his belt and tug it free from its tongue. Her pants were in his way, but the leggings moved easily down over her buttocks. She lifted each cheek that he might keep pulling them. He only had the patience to remove one leg before he was on her.

He palmed her wet core, teasing her slit with a finger. He met her in a fierce kiss, penetrating her with a digit. Feeling the heat of her. Fuck.

She reached between their bodies to grip him, and he hissed. His hips twitched. He moved in time to her strokes.

It was awkward for them both to play and still kiss. But they didn't care. He couldn't have enough of...everything.

"You're so hot," she murmured into his mouth.

He didn't dare say it was only because of the direct, warming sunlight. While he wasn't ice cold, he did tend to be whatever the ambient temperature was, even with his clothes.

"We need protection?" she whispered on his skin as she stroked him.

He was almost tempted to say fuck it and take her against a wall in the shadows. But for the first time, he wanted to feel everything.

The condom went on, and then she guided him into her, her legs locking tight around his shanks as she released her grip. Her sex took over. Squeezing him.

Her heat.

He could barely think. Only move. A slower grind than expected. No hard, rapid-fire thrusts. He just subtly pushed into her sex, rubbing the spot that made her clench each time he stroked it.

Her body met his grind with soft gasps of pleasure. When she came, though, it was with a sharp cry. The best kind that came with all her pelvic muscles tightening.

He came hard and yelled himself.

And was still coming down from his orgasmic

high when he heard Bec whisper, "Should we ask if he's okay?"

"Shh. I don't think they're finished." Sasha didn't exactly speak low.

If he wasn't slipping out of a still pulsing Klementine, he might have snarled something about eating them.

As it was, he'd have a talk about knocking. Not entering!

she'd wager a lot of the specialness in Annie came from her father.

What was Frederick? Because vampire didn't completely cover it.

And she'd just had sex with him.

With a condom. They'd played safe. *I'll be fine. I'm on the pill.*

The baby's mouth worked. The little fire engine about to wail. The bottle she'd heated while ruminating clicked over to ready.

She gave it a quick check and popped it into the baby's mouth. The sight of the milk being guzzled actually soothed her.

Annie might be part vampire, but she drank milk. Canned formula, but still, made for human babies. She didn't crave blood or bite too often, and when she did get impatient and chomped Klementine, her tiny nubs of teeth did no damage.

Which made her wonder if the DNA test that supposedly proved Frederick's parentage was fake. But why would Frederick want to adopt a child so badly he'd go through that kind of effort?

Upon starting the nanny job, she'd hypothesized a few scenarios such as he wanted to groom a human either for later snacking or use as a sex slave. Problem being, she just couldn't see it. Either he should win an award for acting or he truly loved and wanted his daughter.

As for sex... The man didn't have issues in that department. Look at how easily he'd gotten her pants off.

She spent the rest of that afternoon caring for the child, her mind churning. Especially since he never once showed his face.

Did he regret the sex? Would things become awkward?

What if he fired her or had her tossed out?

The more he stayed away, the crazier her thoughts became.

Usually, he tried to find a moment to pop in at least once during the day. She didn't see him until after Annie's bath, which he'd previously declared his favorite time of the day. The baby smelled yummy, as all babies did. She wore footed pajamas, a light pink with happy, sleepy-eyed sloths on them.

As Klementine emerged from the bathroom with Annie, she froze at the sight of Frederick.

He smiled.

Her stomach flipped.

It took her a second to realize the smile probably wasn't for her.

"Here." She held out the baby. "I take it you're here for snuggles."

"I wouldn't miss them." He scooped up Annie. "My princess." He cradled her head and had the softest expression.

It turned fierce when he glanced at Klementine.

Smoldering.

So much for thinking he'd already lost interest.

She fled to her room, leaving him alone with the baby but returned with a bottle. Annie wouldn't go down without one.

He'd taken up a spot in the rocking chair that appeared in the nursery. A bigger, sturdier wooden affair than what was in her room. Obviously brought in for him.

He took the bottle and fed his daughter, rocking and humming something low. Melodic.

She couldn't leave, and so she stared and understood one crucial thing. He'd never hurt that child. But Klementine remained very afraid for her heart.

When the baby bottle was emptied, he easily rolled Annie onto his shoulder, rubbing in a circular motion on her back, waiting for a burp. Amazing what a week could do with comfort levels. He gently placed the baby into the crib. Whispered good night.

Then he pivoted. His gaze narrowing in on her. Her chest tightened as she held her breath.

Neither of them said a word as he led her to her room. Hotter than she recalled. Probably because someone had turned on the gas fireplace

And then she erupted in a lusty heat from his kisses.

She forgot all her trepidation as she embraced him back. She cried out when he laid her on the plush rug in front of the fireplace.

She kept crying out as he spread her thighs and licked her. Licked her until she arched and came against his lips. Then tongue-lashed her clit again until she whimpered.

Only then did he slide his body into her, thrusting slowly. Each jab of his shaft hitting her G-spot. Making her tighten. And squeeze. And gasp.

His lips were pressed against her shoulder, the hard nip of his teeth on skin shiver inducing. And when that pressure pinched, she shattered, coming so hard she left her body for a second and wasn't alone.

A presence surrounded her. Cradled her. Made her feel safe.

Made her stupidly happy.

And while he liked to bite during sex, he never sucked on her or hurt her. On the contrary, the pleasure was unbelievable.

So, she let her guard down, and their affair lasted almost two months before it came crashing down.

## CHAPTER FIFTEEN

SINCE THE BIRTH of his daughter, life had taken on a vibrance and color Frederick had long given up. With his daughter and Klementine, he found happiness. He softened, and his staff noticed it.

"You're looking awfully pleased with yourself, boss," Sasha noted.

"It's a gorgeous day." The sun streamed brightly onto the table, bathing him in its radiance. He felt warm. And hungry.

Going human always demanded food. This morning he'd chosen eggs benedict with orange slices and coffee. Three contrasting flavors. As a vampire, he'd spent centuries drinking blood, sometimes eating raw flesh, and while each vein differed in flavor, they were still very similar. The widening of his diet had led to him putting on five pounds.

Sasha reached in and grabbed a pastry. She'd already been outside for her morning perimeter. Before taking a bite, she said, "Love agrees with you, boss."

The coffee in his mouth sprayed all over his perfect meal. Ruined.

"What the fuck?" He shoved the plates away and glared at Sasha.

"Don't deny it. We can all see it."

"Who is this 'we'?"

"Bec. And a few of the boys."

"And what do they supposedly see?" he asked, dabbing at his pants, trying to ignore that echoing word: love.

"Well, first off, you've been freaking them out with your constant smiling. A few of them think you're secretly plotting our murder."

"Too much work. I'd get you to quit by having you constantly infested with fleas."

The threat brought a snort to Sasha's lips. "As if you'd kill us. You're way too busy being happy. Smiling all the time. Acting gentlemanly. It'd be nauseating if you weren't so horn dogged about it.

Boinking everywhere as if you've discovered a sudden ancestry to bunnies."

"I'm not—That is—" He found himself at a loss of words, wondering how times he and Klementine had actually been caught when they'd indulged in an impromptu lovemaking—

Fuck.

He pushed his plate away. "I can't be in love."

"Why not?"

"Because vampires don't love."

"Says who?" Sasha asked.

"Everybody," he exclaimed. "We are cold-hearted, murderous creatures."

"Bah, you actually kill less people in a year than I do. So, who's the real monster?" Sasha argued.

"I am not arguing about who is more badass again." Last time he'd ended up barely surviving the many, many bottles of booze they drank while debating. "I am also rejecting your claim that I'm in love. It's just a physical thing. And she's convenient." The lie soured his mouth.

"Really? Then you'd be okay with her dating someone else?" Asked with all innocence to cover the slyness of the query.

"No." He growled as impressively as a Lycan.

"But only because then she'd be less available. And we all know it's all about me."

Sasha didn't even try to hide her amusement. "Speaking of available, don't you think she deserves some time off? Kay's been here twenty-four seven for like the last two months." Kay being the name the staff gave Klementine. It was starting to stick. Even he'd found himself using it.

"She hasn't complained."

"How can she when her spare time is spent naked with you? You should give her the day off. Send her into town with Norris."

"No."

"Why not?" Sasha asked. "And think carefully before you reply."

She'd hemmed him into a corner, and she knew it. Jealousy burned hot inside at the thought of Klementine being with someone else. It was wrong.

He couldn't help myself.

His lack of answer led to Sasha exclaiming, "You just proved my point. And I don't know why you're acting like such a coward about it. What's so bad about being in love?"

"She's part Fae."

"And? You're a vampire. I'm a Lycan. Does it really matter?"

It shouldn't. "What if she betrays me?"

"Do you seriously believe she'd do that?" Sasha rolled forward from the wall where she leaned. "You already act like a married couple with a kid. Why not just make it official and put a ring on her finger? Then you could stop playing around and move her into your bedroom."

Marry?

Frederick had done many things in his life, but he'd only married once. He was human at the time, and when he turned, his wife pretended to support him. She'd been the one to lead the enemy to his bed in the dungeon. It didn't end well for them.

But Klementine wasn't Seraphina. She was unlike anyone he'd ever met.

"Package," Bec announced, entering the room, waving it. She'd dyed her platinum streak a hot pink. It went well with the silver jewelry she wore in defiance to the Lycan dislike of it.

As the package hit the table, he winced. "Careful with my meds." Pausing his sunshine trysts with Klementine would suck.

"Relax, boomer," Bec sassed.

"You do realize, in my culture, age is revered, not reviled," he retorted.

"Shouldn't make too much fun of his age. For an old guy, he's got stamina," Sasha interjected.

"True dat," Bec agreed, adding, "I heard Kay holler at least four times last night."

"Four times? Not bad," Sasha uttered with an approving nod.

"It was actually five," he corrected. "And I wish you wouldn't spy on me."

"Then put a ball gag in her mouth. She's loud."

He grinned. "I know." It never ceased to please him how Kay came and came hard each time they were together. On his mouth, his cock, his fingers. And she returned the favor. He'd never been happier, which was when disaster struck.

## CHAPTER SIXTEEN

ALL THEIR SMART devices went off at once. It wasn't a false alarm.

"Perimeter attack," Sasha exclaimed.

During the day. Not really a surprise his enemies would choose high noon, because any other vampire would be weak.

Not this vampire.

"Check with Braedon and make sure the pack is moving into position. Let's hold them back. I don't want anyone reaching the house. I'll go tell Kay to hide with the baby." Because Frederick feared more for them than himself. He leapt the stairs two at a time to find Kay standing in the doorway of her room.

"What's happening? A shutter just slammed down over my window."

Security activated at the first sign of alarm.

"We've got someone testing the fence."

"Someone?" She frowned. "That's kind of vague."

"Most likely goblins."

She predictably exploded. "We're being attacked!"

"It hasn't been confirmed."

"Don't you dare placate me."

"Fine, if you must know, it appears as if we're being invaded. But don't worry, my guards are out there containing the threat. I'll be joining them, but I wanted to first check on you and Annie."

"We're fine. Is she in danger?" She glanced behind her to the nursery door.

"I hope not, but just in case, stay with her in the nursery until I come back for you."

"Where are you going?"

"To keep you and Annie safe."

Her expression went from scared to soft. "Be careful." She kissed him gently, and he almost said it. Almost confessed his feelings.

Later. When he didn't have to rush off.

He trampled down the stairs to find Bec and

Sasha waiting for him by the front door, the only portal not yet locked down.

"Status?" he barked, hitting the main floor, the stone smoothed from passage.

"About thirty or so goblins are hitting the west fence with another twenty or so attempting to climb the south ravine," Bec replied.

"Not likely unless they grow wings." It wasn't just the climb that made it hard. There were other things up that steep face that would get in the way. "What about north and east?"

"Nothing yet," Sasha declared as they went out the front door.

"Do we know what they want?" he asked as they hit the outside air and he took a moment to taste it.

"Nope. But Braedon was planning to grab one and tickle its toes." The kind of "tickling" that would cause screaming, not laughter.

Frederick cocked his head. "Do you smell that?" Wafting down the drive, the scent of goblins. Lots of them. "Are you sure the north is clear?"

"Apparently not. Fuck," Sasha snapped before turning from him and uttering a few sharp yips.

"How many?" he asked, knowing Bec's tracking nose would pinpoint better than his.

He was less than reassured by her. "Lots."

Baying echoed in the distance. Braedon and the wolves were hunting. The full pack wasn't there, although those living off property would have been called in. Would they arrive quick enough? Fifty some goblins, easy enough to handle. But a hundred and fifty? The odds started skewing.

"What do you want to do, boss?" Sasha asked.

Not run, that was for sure. These were goblins after all, and probably a group for hire. If Frederick and the pack could put a dent in their numbers, the goblins might decide their lives were worth more than any contract.

"We need someone to watch the house." Logic dictated he stay behind, but his family was in danger. He didn't want to be the one staying behind. He wanted to fight and protect.

"There's a couple of cars on the road, four minutes out. I can tell them to guard the house."

"Do it." Four minutes with the goblins still far out gave him time to wade in and stop the attack. The house was secured, and nothing short of a tank would easily break in.

"I'll take point." Bec took off running, leaving Sasha to curse and catch up.

Frederick cast a glance at house. Should he

wait for the reinforcements? Four minutes seemed short unless impatience filled you.

He heard a yelp in the distance and couldn't help himself. He shoved away his unease as he followed Bec and Sasha into the woods. His guards had already shifted, a sinuous change from flesh to fur. He envied the ease of their transition. Frederick had other skills, honed over centuries.

He became a thing of shadow, a wraith with clawing fingers and dark teeth. He flowed like a deadly breeze amongst the trunks, aiming for the threat.

Bec uttered an excited yip, and then they were plowing into the invading goblins. Tearing through them like a scythe through wheat chaff.

It was almost too easy. The spilling of their guts. The taking of their heads. These were not great mercenaries. Just petty thugs in the grand scheme, who procreated too quickly.

He couldn't blame them for accepting the wealth the Fae offered if they'd fight for their cause. He did have to wonder if the goblins ever thought the price in lives was worth it.

How much was the prize? Must be high, as they died in big numbers, waves of them. Yelling and tossing themselves uselessly against his claws. As if they had a suicidal plan.

Or wanted to create a distraction. Why, though?

When Frederick realized what it might mean, he fled the battle and raced back to his house to find the door wide open.

Klementine and his baby were gone.

## CHAPTER SEVENTEEN

*WHAT HAVE I DONE?*

The question kept repeating itself, and the answer never failed to horrify.

*I betrayed the man I love.*

Klementine had betrayed Frederick the moment she'd opened the door to her mother, the biological one. Guinevere, High Lady in the Fae court, who, with cold calculation, ensured she produced half-breed children to be her agents in the outside world. A woman who saw nothing wrong with giving birth to children she never intended to keep. Guinevere didn't believe in affection. But criticism? She doled out plenty of that.

*"Stand up straight. You look like a crone."*

*"Do something about that hair. Like find a brush."*

Klementine had long ago run out of tears at the fact she'd never be good enough. It didn't help that Mother Bernice had explained over and over how Klementine and the other abandoned part Fae should be honored the High Lady even chose to acknowledge their existence. Having some Fae blood put her above humans, but lower than the least-favored full Fae.

The class system bothered Klementine almost as much as the fact her mother didn't love her no matter how hard she tried. And oh, how she used to try to earn that approval.

Nothing ever ranked as good enough. So why had Klementine opened that door? She knew nothing good would come of it.

When the attack started, she'd planned to lock herself in the nursery with Annie and not come out until Frederick returned, only she paused at the threshold. If someone broke in, the nursery would probably be the first place they'd go. Not to mention it would be a deathtrap if a fire was started.

Rather than lock herself in, she went where assassins and thieves would probably avoid—the half-bath on the main floor, tucked under the stairs. Wide enough she could sit on the floor with the baby and pretend poorly that she wasn't frightened.

What felt like an hour showed as two minutes since he'd left. What if Fred didn't come back?

At three minutes, she crept out from under the stairs and listened. Nothing. She carried Annie to the front door and lay her ear on it.

It was locked, and yet she knew she could escape if needed. The lockdown was meant to keep people out, not in.

So long as she didn't open it, she'd be safe.

At four minutes, she'd worn a hole in the tile and vowed she'd die protecting the baby if someone managed to smash their way inside.

At five minutes she got a text from High Lady Guinevere. Her mother.

*Open the door.*

Klementine glanced at the thick portal as if she could see through it. She didn't doubt Guinevere stood outside, but she did wonder why she'd come.

Klementine's fingers flew as she texted, *Are you the one attacking Frederick?*

A pause before the next reply. *Open the door.*

In other words, yes.

Someone had betrayed Klementine. Who? Had to be Bernice. Way to make her regret telling her foster mom about Coralline's baby and the possible daddy. Bernice must have spilled the news, and now, her mother, for the first time in her life and with incredibly bad timing, wanted to see her and might kill Frederick in the attempt.

She had to do something.

*Call off the attack. I'm fine,* Klementine typed. Send.

Immediately, the little dots bounced as her mother typed a reply. *Open the door and prove it.*

Then a second later. *Bring the child.*

The insistence had Klementine biting her lip. She had to ask. *Are you planning to hurt Anemone?*

*I would never harm a child.*

Wouldn't she, though? After all, she'd dumped all her half-human children on Bernice, who, at times, was less a motherly figure and more like a strict warden. She'd softened as she hit her late sixties. Not that Coralline ever met that Bernice. Coralline had the courage to rebel at a younger age, whereas Klementine kept seeking approval, which was why she opened the door.

Being a mature woman now, she'd talk to her mother and make her understand that while she appreciated that Guinevere cared enough to mount a rescue, it wasn't necessary. Maybe this would be a starting point for something real.

Ha.

She knew better. Her mother didn't have a soft bone in her body, but she did have a vindictive one. Not opening wasn't an option. Disobedience would be met with punishment otherwise.

Guinevere stood on the porch dressed all in white, the material vibrant and reflecting light. Flanking her were two bowmen armed with the latest in electrical bolts. The power packs gave them access to a thousand bolts per quiver, and they could shoot them fast enough to use them all. Or so she'd heard. The half-Fae guy she'd tried to date a while back had gushed about them.

"My lady." Klementine knew better than to avoid the half-curtsy and dip of her head. "What are you doing here?"

"Rescuing you from that vampire!" Mother exclaimed as if she'd suddenly discovered she had one noble bone, probably in her little toe.

"I don't need rescuing, which you'd know if you'd called first. Apparently, you know my number." Guinevere just usually chose to ignore it.

"Don't get sassy. Bad enough I'm too late. You were seen kissing *him*." Ooh, that inflection.

Klementine's cheeks heated as she sputtered, "Fred is not what you think."

"Frederick Thibodeaux is exactly what I think. A murdering vampire who is using you. Look at you, dazzled by a monster. And who knows what he has in store for this child."

"He loves Annie," she defended.

"Vampires can't love. They only destroy." An ironic statement, given all her mother's machinations outside the Fae kingdom.

Did Fred love her? He'd never said anything. But then again, neither had she.

Fingers snapped. "Let's go. We don't have time to waste. It's costing me a fortune to delay the reinforcements." Guinevere moved, not waiting to see if she followed.

Klementine wondered if she could slam the door shut in time. As she did, one of the bowmen shoved his foot in the closing wedge. And shoved. Protecting the baby with her arms, Klementine stumbled and landed on her ass, hard.

The bowman stood over her, aiming a sizzling bolt as Annie began to cry.

Mother appeared behind him and shook her

head. "Did you really think you had another option?"

"Let me put the baby in her room so she's safe first."

A brow arched. "You're bringing the child."

"She's innocent."

"She's got Fae blood. She comes with us."

Fred would be crushed—if he lived. "We'll come, but only if you call off your attack."

"This is not a negotiation. I am stopping nothing. And I can't believe you'd even ask," Guinevere hotly exclaimed. "Snap out of it. Resist his evil spell."

As Klementine's lips moved to say, *He's not evil,* she had to wonder. Could her mother be right? Had he duped her?

Guinevere lost all semblance of patience. "Either you get moving or I won't be responsible for what happens when my men teach you a lesson in obedience."

The bowmen glanced at each other, but she had no doubt they'd obey. What choice did she have? With great reluctance—*I'm so sorry*—she tucked Annie close and left the house. The safety she'd ruined.

In the distance, she could hear baying and

snarling. A battle raged, and Frederick probably fought in the midst of it. Fought because of her.

She should have stayed away from him because, in the end, her Fae blood betrayed him.

A quiver went through her as she imagined his rage—and hurt—when he discovered them gone. While she'd originally planned to steal Annie when she got a chance, now the very idea sickened her.

She wished she could fight, but her mother wouldn't hesitate to hurt. She couldn't risk Annie.

Perhaps once she got an audience at the Fae Court, she could explain how Frederick differed from other vampires, and not just because he could walk in the sun. She'd argue his case. Make them see he wasn't a threat.

She'd bring him Annie and safety as an apology.

That fantasy shattered the moment she arrived in the Fae kingdom and her mother had her locked away.

## CHAPTER EIGHTEEN

KLEMENTINE WAS TOSSED INTO A CELL, albeit a generous one, at the top of the tower wide enough to pace but too high to escape.

It was clear Guinevere had no interest in the truth. Nor had she suddenly grown a maternal bone. She'd kidnapped Klementine and Annie to use as leverage in her campaign to elevate her position at court.

Tricked. It soured Klementine's stomach, especially since she became a virtual prisoner in the one place she'd long considered paradise but had never been allowed to visit.

She was finally in Solis, the Fae Kingdom, where magic filled the very fabric of the place, everything thrived, and building wasn't just practical but an art. A massive kingdom that every half-Fae dreamed of seeing. Only a lucky few ever got to stay in the land where the sun always shone. The last place a vampire could go to.

And not a great place for a vampire's lover and his baby. The Fae attending to her made no attempt to mask their disdain. She could have screamed how wrong they were. Instead, she ignored them. Closed-minded people would believe what they wanted. She had no time to waste on them.

She saw no one else other than the guard who opened the door for whoever brought her a meal. She had a cramped area for doing her business, the water barely trickling, the toilet missing its seat.

She had windows with bars across them. A few of them were loose enough she might be able to work them free, giving her a glimpse of the forbidden city. A city she'd been told eclipsed all others in beauty.

At one time, it must have been elegant and grand, but she couldn't help but notice the shabbiness overtaking the city. As if people had stopped caring.

Maybe they had. After all, the Fae queen had

left, with no reason, no warning, and her people were losing faith, especially with Klementine's despot mother at the helm.

Three days into her imprisonment, Klementine knew she had to do something.

But what? Alone, she might have dared the climb from her window and escaped, but she couldn't leave Annie behind. She needed help, but everyone here was loyal to—and very scared of—Guinevere, their current unelected ruler. Given her short temper, no one liked to cross her.

Still, when Bernice came to check on their welfare, Klementine knew she had to give it a try. "Hey, Mother B." She offered a wan smile.

Bernice filled the room as she asked, "How are you and the baby doing?"

"We're in a cell. How do you think we're doing? Why did you rat me out?" She boldly went on the offensive.

"You left me no choice. Living with a vampire."

"Then you should have talked to me. Not tattled to my mother."

"She needed to know."

"Did she need to know about Annie, too?" Klementine accused.

Bernice wouldn't meet her gaze. "I didn't mean to tell her. It was an accident."

"An accident that stole a child from her father. Fred needs to know Annie is okay."

"Who cares what that evil creature feels?" Bernice *tsked* as she checked over Coralline's baby, ticking the bottoms of feet for reaction, the belly for giggles.

"Fred is not evil. He loves Annie. More than Guinevere loves me," Klementine added for good measure.

Bernice eyed her. "Your mother isn't one to waste time on affection. At her age, she's seen too many of her children die."

"Doesn't it bother you that she hates us?" A reminder of their familial tie.

"She doesn't hate me," Bernice declared.

Stupid, mindless loyalty. "You're only saying that because she pays your bills."

Which was when Klementine got the idea. She talked for fifteen minutes straight but didn't know if she got through to Bernice. She could only wait and see if the seed she'd planted bore fruit.

## CHAPTER NINETEEN

ANNIE AND KAY WERE GONE. Frederick spent the days after their disappearance in a mindless rage. He'd tracked them a hundred times. Watched the security video inside the front hall and outside his front door, over and over. Had time to get over his disbelief that Kay would open the door and betray him to Guinevere, the bane of his existence since he'd spurned her advances.

His heart shattered as his enemy dared threaten the two people most precious to him. He cracked as he heard Kay's soft murmur before she was escorted away, *"I'm so sorry."*

So was he. The first time he watched and heard, he couldn't forgive her. He didn't want to forgive her. He would have killed her if he'd found her. By the hundredth time watching, he was ready to accept Kay hadn't wanted to be abducted. She'd tried to leave the baby behind.

Evil didn't listen.

On day five of heavy drinking and violence—because everyone who'd slighted him in the last decade got to feel his vengeance—Sasha confronted him. "How long you going to mope like a dumped bitch before you do something?"

"What can I do? They vanished into thin fucking air."

They'd searched and searched, only to remain stymied. Guinevere and her cohorts had walked out of the forest as if they'd just appeared there. They left the same way, taking Kay and Annie with them. The only clue? A ring of clover, which Bec claimed acted as a conduit for fairy magic. Also known as a doorway to the Fae kingdom, a place forbidden to him.

"They're not dead," Sasha insisted.

"How can you be so sure?" he growled. Guinevere hated him. What would she do to his daughter? The idea he might have failed to protect haunted him.

"I know they're alive because someone

approached us. Sold us information. Has more if you're willing to meet the price."

The statement lifted his heavy head. "Who is this person?"

"Calls herself Bernice. Says she was Kay's guardian growing up."

"Her foster mother," he murmured. He'd read about her in a report, and Kay had revealed chunks of her childhood to him. But she'd never talked about her real mother. An oversight or had she hidden the truth on purpose?

"She says that Kay and the baby are fine, but not happy about being prisoners."

His elation at their being alive faded as he understood their position. "They're holding them hostage?" He roused from his seat, anger burning away the effects of alcohol.

"Yes. A different informant has confirmed her information and added that Guinevere's recent confrontation with you is part of her push to have Queen Mab declared dead so she can take the throne."

"Mab is still missing?" She'd ruled the Fae for as long as anyone could remember.

"More than a century now and Guinevere tires

of her title of High Lady and seeks a crown." Sasha had done some digging.

The knowledge didn't surprise him. He glanced at Sasha. "What else did Bernice tell you? Because I assume you paid her?"

Sasha grimaced. "After Bernice extorted a large sum, she told us Klementine and the baby are being held in Solis, which could be a few places according to Google."

"The Solis she speaks of is not on any map." And he already knew they'd taken his child there.

The one place he couldn't follow. Solis, the land of perpetual sun, didn't exist on the same plane as the rest of them. Best as he could understand, Solis was an invisible pocket kingdom, constantly in motion, following the sun. Its entrance was a closely guarded secret known to Fae only.

"I'm sure if we offer the right amount, she'll show us how to get there."

"Going there is suicide. I might as well cut my own head off now," he muttered. A place of pure sunshine? Could his body handle it?

Just in case, he injected a serum from his newest batch. It burned going in, and he hissed. Usually, he waited until the last dose wore off. But he didn't have a choice. He couldn't have his protection fading while he was inside Solis, because he was taking his daughter back. "Pay her whatever she asks and find out how we get in."

"We gonna raid fairy land?" Bec's eyes widened. "Sweet."

"I'd rather not go to war but will if I have to. This has to stop," he declared.

"If we're going after the fairies, we need allies." Sasha remained practical.

"He's got us," Bec reminded, thumping her chest.

"The pack isn't enough if we're going to invade Fairyland," Sasha argued.

"We don't have the numbers to invade, and I don't really want to see that many lives lost," Frederick interjected. It was one thing to kill those who came against him, but to wage a war against an entire species? There had to be a less bloody way.

It hit him with an elegance he couldn't resist.

"Fuel my jet," he said.

"Are we going somewhere?" Sasha asked.

"I know how we're going to get both my girls back. But we'll need to convince someone to help us first."

And last he'd heard, they were living in Alaska.

## CHAPTER TWENTY

A KNOCK at the door preceded a palace guard. Klementine had dealt with this one before. Left the experience wanting to slap him and mock him for his outfit. He wore a tight-fitting silvery shirt tucked into snug breeches. All the uniforms appeared a few sizes too small. Guinevere's decision. Funny how the female guards all got full-length, baggy pants.

The guard's pointed ears poked artfully between his carefully combed and parted long blond hair. "You are to accompany me at once."

Klementine rose from the carpet where she'd been playing with Annie. "Accompany you where?"

"The amphitheatre. The High Lady has commanded your presence, along with the child." That would be a first since her arrival.

"Why?" she asked.

"It's not up to you to question."

She crossed her arms. "Given the last time I obeyed resulted in me and an innocent child locked away, I'd say I have reason to ask." She'd given up on polite a few days ago. Let them all face what they were doing. Did no one see her mother's power-hungry madness?

For a moment his nostrils flared before he huffed. "There's a stranger making his way to the city."

She blinked. "Who is it? Do you know a name?"

The guard shrugged. "Can't recall. But people are saying it's a vampire."

Her heart began beating faster. "Has he been harmed?"

"Nope. Someone told the leech to come under a silver banner and demand safe passage."

The Fae version of the humans' white flag. It meant they couldn't harm him. Although she wouldn't put it past Guinevere to try.

"Give me a second to sling the baby and grab a

bottle." At least she didn't lack for amenities in Solis. Although, rather than electronics, magic fueled most things over here.

Annie grabbed for Klementine's hair as she snuggled her into the fabric band. The familiar movement didn't distract as she wondered what possessed Fred to walk into enemy territory. Guinevere would kill him if given a chance. Hadn't Bernice told him she had a plan?

She'd described it in great detail. She was going to pretend she hated Frederick and claim he'd bespelled her. Then, when her mother lowered her guard, Klementine would ask to live with Bernice so as to not be a bother. Once there, she'd be able to contact Frederick and return Annie to him. It would only be a few weeks, months at the most, surely.

She should have known Frederick's impatience would drive him to act sooner.

The guard led her right to the amphitheatre, shaped from the stone that formed the heart of Solis. The floor was polished and glowing bright. The innermost circle held the throne, over which the sun always hung. A sun that never moved. Never dimmed.

How Klementine missed the shadows of night.

The brightness wasn't helped by the white, silver, and pale gold worn by everyone. Blinding, really. Annie complained and turned her face into Klementine.

"I know, baby. If you ask me, all this sunshine is torture."

She was brought to stand in the wings of the dais. Her mother already sat on her throne, flanked by her loyal subjects. Her archers. A few hand-maidens.

The seats were filled with Fae, dressed too bright to stare at for long. They whispered and hummed. If she strained, she could hear them.

*"...can't believe the High Lady hasn't killed him."*

*"Even she doesn't dare break the laws of safe passage."*

*"Did you hear she's keeping a half-breed and her kid locked in the tower?"*

*"I hear the baby is a monster and ate the father."*

There was a time Klementine would have heard it and believed it. Because believing a rumor was easier than finding out the truth.

She knew better now. She knew Frederick wasn't the real monster here, and that would cost him his life.

Apparently, he didn't get that message. He didn't act as if he walked to his doom. He strutted as if he had every right to enter Solis. He didn't flinch in the sun's rays. Didn't do anything at all but stand tall. Look confidant. Handsome. All that, and yet not once did he look her way.

The murmurs shifted. *"He can't be a vampire. What is he?"*

Because, in that moment, he appeared very human except for one thing.

Frederick showed no fear, as if he didn't grasp the odds arrayed against him. It didn't go unnoticed. The hushed whispers faded and then stopped completely as he remained in a staring competition with High Lady Guinevere. Everyone waited for one of them to break the silence.

The High Lady cracked first. "What do you here, foul creature? This place isn't allowed to your kind."

"Thank you for the reminder that *my kind*," he inflected, "usually can't step one foot inside without fertilizing your lovely grassy plains."

"Vampires aren't meant to walk in the sun," Guinevere stated.

"I wouldn't have to if you'd not stolen something of mine. I've come for my daughter."

As he stated it, Klementine knew it was logical. Of course, he'd not come for her. It still hurt.

"Anemone is not your daughter." Guinevere waved a hand as if that were the end of it.

Frederick snorted. "You know she is, and that's why you took her. Still peeved I wouldn't sleep with you? Get over it."

There was an audible sound from the crowd. He'd just shamed Guinevere, and Klementine bit her lip as she imagined her reaction.

It proved icy cold. "As if I'd ever abase myself. I have more standards than my bastard."

Ouch. Klementine felt that insult.

"Which leads me to my second demand. Along with my daughter, you will also give me Klementine."

Was it a good thing he wanted her or bad? Either way her breath halted in her lungs. When his gaze met hers finally, it smoldered. His expression promised they were good. Or so she assumed, given he winked then faced forward again.

What was he doing?

"You want her, take her." Guinevere waved a hand as if her own child were beneath her. "She's useless to me. But the child stays."

"I never said this was a negotiation." Was it

intentional he used Guinevere's own words, which she'd spoken in his house? "Don't make me tear this kingdom apart to take back what you stole."

"We stole nothing." Guinevere slapped her hand on the armrest of her ornate throne. "They are Fae."

"They are *mine*."

Possessive. Growled and rumbly. A claim that had weight behind it. Power, and those in the amphitheatre felt it. Shifted nervously.

Guinevere chose to ignore the danger. "I tire of your bleating. Archers, rid the court of him."

"High Lady, he's under the truce flag." The bowman with the purple ribbon around his arm lowered his weapon rather than fire.

"He's an enemy of this court." Guinevere flung out a hand, and the magic, so strong in this place, fired like a missile.

Frederick put up a hand, and the purple bolt of lightning hit his palm, sizzling, bringing a wince to his lips. He hissed with the pain.

The crowd went silent except for one voice who dared to shout-whisper, "How come he's not dead?"

A good question, which Klementine didn't get an answer to because that was when Anemone, asleep in the sling across her chest, woke. Stretched, yawned, and then bellowed.

"Da!"

No one could miss the softening of Fred's face when he heard Annie say his name. His baby had said her first word. His name.

And what did her stupid mother scream?

"Klementine, kill the child!"

CHAPTER TWENTY-ONE

THE VIOLENT, insane command dropped like a bomb in the silent amphitheatre. Klementine couldn't believe Guinevere had said it.

Frederick reacted. "Don't you dare hurt my daughter!"

As if she ever would. Klementine shoved through the courtesans watching the byplay until she emerged in a clear spot halfway between Frederick and Guinevere.

She kept a hand tucked around the baby. "Are you insane? I am not hurting Annie or anyone else for that matter."

"Useless garbage. I should have left you behind for him to kill," her mother hissed.

Way to remind him of her betrayal. "Trust me when I say I wish I'd never opened that door. My mistake in thinking you had a heart." Let this be the final time she learned that hard lesson.

"Put her back in her cell," Guinevere barked.

Only to have Frederick counter with, "Whoever touches her will die first." A ridiculous threat, given the many soldiers arraigned against him, and yet, he rolled up his sleeves as if he had all the time in the world.

"And what will you do, vampire?" Guinevere said with a massive sneer. Could anyone else feel the ominous foreboding in the air? "You are here alone. In my court. I am the one in control." She waved a hand. "Shoot him."

Her bowmen instead lay down their weapons. The purple beribboned one adding, "We won't spill blood under a truce flag."

"I'll remember your betrayal. A good thing I have an army at my beck and call."

"About your army," Frederick interjected. "The thing about mercenaries, especially the goblins, is they'll work for whoever pays the best price." He smiled. "Guess who was willing to go highest."

The bold claim had the tenor of the crowd

shifting to fear. Despite the sun shining, a chill fell over everyone.

"What a waste of money given it's too late to save you." Guinevere suddenly regained confidence, and it took Klementine a second to realize Frederick was smoking, as in his skin literally steamed. Guinevere cackled. "I wondered how long you would last."

Frederick quickly understood the implication. "The serum delivered to my house. You tampered with it."

"Wasn't hard to intercept it. Did you really think we wouldn't find out? Day-walking vampires?" She sneered. "That kind of perversion can't be allowed."

As Frederick's skin continued to flush and he wobbled, he said, "Guess it's a good thing I made sure others were told of the secret."

"You what?" Guinevere stood finally and ogled him in shock.

Frederick smiled even as pain took him to his knees, his skin pale and blurred from the steam rising. "It didn't seem right to hoard the secret, so I sold it to a few of my friends. It's how I managed to buy your army. How's it feel to know you're not so safe anymore?"

"You can't do that!" Guinevere exclaimed. "Solis is for the Fae only."

"Only because no one has ever tried to take it from you."

"You wouldn't dare!" she snarled

"I will since you decided to meddle with my life on Earth. I'd say it's about time you understood what it's like to struggle to survive."

"You doom the innocent." As if Guinevere cared.

"No, you did. I would do anything for love." As he uttered that in a final gasp, he shimmered something fierce, but even through his evident pain, he saw Klementine and smiled. Mouthed impossible words.

*I love you.*

A claim that gave her courage. She lifted her chin and whirled to confront her mother. "Help him."

"He shouldn't have come."

"You didn't give him a choice. You stole his child."

"And he took you. I'd say it was fair turn-about."

"Don't even try to pull that crap," Klementine sassed, wagging a finger. "We all know you didn't come after me because you gave a rat's ass. You wanted leverage."

"And?"

"Annie is innocent in all this."

"Which is why, being the benevolent ruler I am, she'll be handed over to Bernice for raising," Guinevere said.

"Like hell she will. She stays with me." Klementine lifted her chin.

"And I say she doesn't."

"My name is on her birth certificate, so unless you're planning to kill me, if Frederick dies, I get custody." Fred had done it without telling her, presenting the documents with a shy smile and a sheepish claim of, "*If something were to happen, she'll be yours without a hassle.*"

"You would dare defy me?" Guinevere seemed more amused than anything.

"Someone has to say no to your madness."

"Madness. Says the half-breed who doesn't understand. If anyone does, it won't be a half-breed like you. Seize her! No wonder you're not worthy of my regard. Toss her into the outer world. But first, bring the child to me."

Klementine clutched Annie to her. "No."

Everything was unravelling. She couldn't hand the baby over. But she didn't see an escape.

She felt a sudden coolness that quelled her panic a moment before Frederick's voice emerged, smooth as silk and yet loud enough to carry. "I warned you not to fuck with me. Now you pay the price."

## CHAPTER TWENTY-TWO

WHEN FREDERICK'S skin had begun to prickle, disbelief and rage filled him. How unfair. To be so close to those he loved, only to be betrayed by a weakness in his body.

As the heat rose inside him, he honestly thought he'd die. It was why he'd mouthed *I love you* to Klementine. Saw her eyes brimming with tears as her lips moved in reply. *Me too.*

He hit his knees and could barely hear Klementine arguing for his life. Fighting for him.

The burning within scorched everything, and when there was nothing left to consume, he turned cold, his temperature dropping fast. When he thought he might shatter, something inside him exploded. It left him feeling …rather good as a matter of fact.

He took everyone by surprise when he came to stand by Klementine's side.

Especially the High Lady, gaping on her throne. "You should be dead!"

He held out his hand and turned it. "More like I'm finally truly immune. Thank you." Said with a lot of teeth.

"No. Take his head." She surged forward. Alone. Guinevere stumbled to a halt when she saw her soldiers kept their hands tucked behind their backs.

He might have had something to do with their relaxed stance. Despite the hot sun baking into him, he felt strong. Stronger than usual. The power within palpable. As if he could touch the shadows just out of sight.

So he did. He grabbed the darkness and pulled it around himself to horrified gasps.

"What are you doing?" Guinevere exclaimed.

"Giving you one last chance to make this right, or I signal my army. Right after I turn this place into night." He thrust his hand, and a cloak of shadow spread out, causing a few screams.

"You wouldn't dare."

"Try me and see," he taunted right back.

In the silence that followed, a single clap thundered. The noise drew all gazes, and the ground shook as every jaw hit it at once.

In strode Queen Mab, wearing a plaid shirt layered over cargo pants tucked into scuffed combat boots. Her hair was drawn back in a fat braid. She looked like an outdoorswoman, but that impression didn't last. With each step, something shifted in her appearance until she'd flipped into pure rose gold: thigh-high boots, a mini skirt and a crop top that showed off a smooth stomach with no belly button. Given the queen's age, there had long been speculation that, as the first Fae, she'd not been born like the rest of them. A person who ended up dying of a horrible accident had once even surmised she'd hatched from an egg.

Whatever her origin, Queen Mab had been missing for over a century. During that time, Guinevere spent a few decades of maneuvering to become the Highest Lady and began vying for the final prize, the throne.

The funny thing? Frederick would have let Guinevere have it. Would have never gone to Alaska to bug an old friend. But still mad at being jilted, Guinevere had to go and poke the vampire with a stick.

"*Mab.*" People prayed her name as they hit the ground on their knees and genuflected.

Klementine kept her gaze on her mother, Annie tucked into her chest. She pressed into Frederick, cradling into the support of his arm. She glanced at him. "Take Annie and run."

"Don't worry," he whispered into her hair.

"You don't understand. This is bad. Guinevere won't give up the power without a fight."

"I think Mab's counting on that," was his reply as the two women got within arm's length.

Guinevere stood defiantly in front of the throne. Without a seeming care, a casual Mab prowled through those who flanked the High Lady.

She stared more than a few of them down. None held her gaze. One fainted. Another threw themselves prostate and blubbered, "My queen."

Sensing her power slipping, Guinevere blustered. "You might as well turn around and leave. No one wants you. You walked away from us. Abandoned your duty. I'm the one in charge now." Guinevere tried to sound bold, but no one voiced any support.

Mab looked around and made a moue of

displeasure. "Leave for a little bit of me time and I come back to find you trying to eradicate our kind." Queen Mab sniffed. "Really, Guinevere. When are you going to grow up?"

"I did what had to be done. What you couldn't do."

"I never kidnapped and threatened children. Your own flesh and blood? Really?" Mab still maintained the same even tone, and yet the fear in the amphitheatre grew.

"She's weak. Obviously. Look at her, conspiring with a vampire." Guinevere pointed.

Klementine stood taller. Confidant. Then out of her mouth came the most incredible thing. "Fred is a better person than you'll ever be."

He wanted to kiss her. But first, they still needed to leave here alive.

Mab arched a brow. "Knowing Frederick, I don't know if I'd go quite that far."

"Traitor," Guinevere hissed. "Both of you. You abandoned us. Left without a care or instruction."

"All you had to do was not be an asshole, Guinevere." Mab didn't spare the language or tone.

"I'm not the one you should be lecturing. What about Klementine? Spreading her legs for our enemy. Just like Coralline. She should have listened to me when I told her to get an abortion."

"You knew she was pregnant?" Klementine latched onto the admission.

"Can you believe she was proud of it?" Guinevere sneered. "She didn't care at all about the shame."

"Ah yes. Shame." Mab shook her head. "Funny you should mention it, because you definitely don't understand it. Did you think no one would realize the role you played in making that child an orphan?" Mab cast a warm gaze on Annie. She always did have a soft spot for the small and innocent.

It was Klementine who whispered, "You killed Coralline?"

"By accident. She wouldn't get in the car." Guinevere shrugged as if it weren't of import.

But Klementine screeched, "You murdered Cora."

"Coralline wouldn't listen and do what I—"

"Enough." With a wave of her hand, Mab silenced Guinevere. "You are a disgrace to our kind and obviously need some time to reflect on your actions. Perhaps a century or two alone will do you some good." Mab snapped her fingers, and Guinevere disappeared.

Mab ascended the dais and turned to face the amphitheatre with a smile. "Anyone else in need of solitude? I know a great remote place in Alaska." Not a single person moved. Or breathed. "Are you sure? I don't mind sending you."

Dead silence.

"Good. Let Guinevere's fate be a reminder to you all. Fae don't harm Fae. And there is only one queen."

*"Mab."* Everyone hummed her name as if on cue, widening her smile.

Turning to glance at her throne, Mab grimaced. "Hideous and uncomfortable." She waved her hand and replaced it with something more basic. A fabric-covered recliner. She sat in it, kicked out the footrest, and sighed. "That's better."

In the quiet that followed, it was Frederick who drawled, "You took your sweet time."

## CHAPTER TWENTY-THREE

WHEN FREDERICK ROSE from the dead, Klementine sagged in relief. But that was short-lived, as the fabled Queen Mab returned and, with a snap of her fingers, sentenced Guinevere to isolation.

With that kind of power, and willingness to banish a highly placed Fae, what would she do to Frederick?

Worried for his safety, Klementine shifted to stand in front of him just as the idiot accused the queen of taking too long.

Mab replied, "Maybe you shouldn't have rushed in then. What happened to the plan?"

He shrugged. "I got impatient."

"Wait a second." Klementine shifted against him. "You know each other?"

"For centuries now. Freddy and I are old friends," Mab purred, rousing Klementine's jealousy. How well had they known each other?

As if reading her mind, Frederick stated firmly, "We're simply friends."

"Not for lack of trying." Mab laughed, a deep sound that was both beautiful and terrible at once. Her gaze lit on Klementine. "You're new since I was last at Court."

"Klementine, Your Majesty." She curtsied.

"Sorry about your mother."

"That makes two of us, Your Majesty."

"Call me Mab. After all, you and I are about to become close. Let me see the baby."

Klementine glanced at Frederick, whose jaw appeared taut, but he nodded. She ascended the steps and handed over Annie to the queen who said, "Let it be known that Anemone Starfish hyphen Thibodeaux is under my direct protection. I claim her as my granddaughter. A hand raised against her is a hand raised against me. And we would do well to remember what a bad idea that is."

The queen stood and held the baby as her gaze

tracked over the crowd before handing her back. "Take good care of Annie."

"I will, Your Majesty."

"You are the one Freddy told me about," Mab stated, tilting her head. "The reason he disturbed my retreat."

"I told you she was special," he said.

The queen eyed Klementine more intently, capturing her with a kaleidoscope stare that left her dizzy and breathless. Then Mab asked, "Do you wish to depart with Frederick?"

Before she could reply, a voice yelled, "He's a vampire!"

*Pop.* Mab only had to aim a finger.

"Anyone else have a problem with my guest?" No more objections occurred. "Now answer me truthfully, Klementine. Would you like to stay in Solis as my handmaiden or return to Earth with the vampire?"

The newly returned queen offered her the highest honor, and yet Klementine wanted only one thing. "I'd like to go home, Your Majesty."

"Then go you shall." Mab smiled at Frederick. "You are free to depart unless you'd like to stay. Our wine is most excellent."

He arched a brow. "I've heard it's so addictive that people never want to leave. I'll pass."

Mab laughed, and Klementine noticed her sharp teeth. "Pity. Having you around would have made things more interesting."

"Sorry to disappoint."

"Who says I'm disappointed? We are not done, old friend. Not by a long shot. After all, I am Annie's grandmother."

Before Klementine could wonder what that meant, the baby decided she'd had enough. With a yodel to wake the dead, she began to protest.

"Goodness, she's got good lungs," Mab declared.

Klementine could only helplessly shrug. "She's hungry."

"Aren't we all!" Mab snapped her fingers. "Who is ready for a feast?"

The amphitheater suddenly sported tables laden with food, much of it still in the containers from the restaurants Mab had stolen it from. As the crowd oohed and aahed, Mab focused once more on Klementine. "You're free to go."

Klementine gave a short dip and fled back down the stairs straight to Frederick, who swept an arm around her. "That was a little intense. Let's go." They exited, Frederick keeping a firm grip on her until they were outside the amphitheatre.

She tried to speak. "Sorry, I—"

"I already know. We should leave before Mab changes her mind and decides we should stay."

"Would she really? I thought she was your friend."

"It took me two days of sweet talking before she'd say yes to us leaving here together. She originally planned to keep you and the baby. Then just you."

"Why me?"

"Because she was really pissed at what your mother did."

"Are you saying you found Mab and brought her back to save us?"

He nodded as they headed into the forest outside the Fae kingdom. "When Bernice told us where you were being held, Sasha reminded me I'd need help if I wanted to escape with my head intact."

"Which was why you hired the goblins."

"I hired them mostly to keep them out of the way. But it occurred to me that, short of killing Guinevere and her supporters, even if I rescued you, we'd have problems."

"So you went and found the missing Fae queen."

"Not so much missing as taking a break. When you live a long time, you go through periods where you crave the silence."

"I'm not quiet," she stupidly reminded him.

His arm around her tightened as they stepped into a ring of mushrooms, avoiding the little blue creatures shaking their fists at them. "I like the way you talk to me. It's part of why I love you."

Before she could speak, they were stepping out into the real world—the woods outside his chateau to be exact—in a different ring of mushrooms, which Sasha and Bec immediately destroyed along with anything else that even so much as looked as if it might be a fairy doorway.

At Klementine's arched brow, he said, "I won't let you and Annie be hurt or kidnapped again."

CHAPTER TWENTY-FOUR

AS THEY ENTERED HIS FORTRESS, Frederick couldn't believe it had worked. He'd not only emerged unscathed, he had both Anemone and Klementine with him.

His calculated risk in tracking down the not always entirely sane Fae queen paid off even if it cost him a promise—"*In the future, I will ask a favor of you...*" He hoped the price she demanded was one he could pay.

Only when they were inside his chateau did he almost breathe. And then he didn't even try to catch a breath as he tugged Klementine close and kissed her. Not as passionately as he would have liked because the baby remained in her arms but hard enough that she panted and regarded him with shining eyes.

"Fred, I—"

"Waaah!" Annie was done.

"Let's handle Annie first."

They took the wailing baby to the nursery, where he paced and bounced her while Klementine prepped a bottle. Only once Annie was slumbering in her crib, and they'd left her room did he take Klementine by the hand and draw her to him.

Hugged her and hugged her. Finally sighing. "I was so worried."

Tears pricked her eyes. "I'm sorry. I should have never opened the door."

"No, you shouldn't have," he admonished but softened it with, "Anyone would have, though. How could you know such perfidy existed in her heart?"

"I knew. I just refused to see it." She leaned into him. "I thought I'd never see you again."

He tilted her chin. "I would do anything for you."

"I love you," she told him, and he'd never heard anything more beautiful and daunting.

He lifted her and brought her to the bed, lying her down on it then slowly stripping her. Baring her to his gaze. Not that the exterior truly mattered. Intimacy was the sexiest thing for him.

Acceptance.

A certainty that she was the missing part of his soul. The one to make him complete.

He worshipped her despite her hot pleas. He kissed her lips, her jaw, her neck. He lavished attention on her breasts, kissing them. Sucking at those berry-ripe nipples. Tugging them drew her cries.

Between her thighs, his fingers found wet dampness. He knelt and teased her lips apart, tasting of the ambrosia, reveling in how she cried out and writhed.

Only when she came did his body cover hers, his shaft sliding into her pulsating heat, plunging deep enough to draw a cry. He took his time grinding into her, the tip of him rubbing against her sweet spot, taking her higher and higher. Tightening her until she clawed at him. Panted.

Dug her nails into his back.

Only then did he bite her, driving her into numerous orgasms even as his own wrung him dry. Left him heaving atop her.

Loving her.

Needing her.

There was no light when she was gone.

Which might be why he was desperate and had her again. And again, until they both slept deeply. Enough that when the baby woke for her middle-of-the-night bottle, there was whispering and shhing as his guards slipped in to care for Annie.

Even as Bec complained, "I am not changing a dirty diaper."

And Sasha replied, "Better get used it. The way they're going, we should expect a litter soon."

"Think they'd let me keep one?"

The next day, he moved his new fiancée into his bedroom, where he had a lock, soundproof walls—and no interruptions.

EPILOGUE

AS IT TURNED OUT, the serum Frederick sold to his friends didn't work well at all with the young vampires. Even some of the older ones required more applications than they liked, which they only grumbled a little bit about. Some sun was better than none.

As for Frederick, while still a vampire, he became very human when in UV light. The biggest change being he no longer needed to inject himself with the serum. Whether he'd just taken enough to change permanently, or because of Mab's magic, he didn't know. Although he suspected the latter because there was no denying the Fae queen had taken an interest in him, and his family.

Mab turned into a frequent visitor, and if one ignored how the ground sometimes trembled when she got excited, she provided an interesting friend for his wife and a powerful ally for his daughter. No one dared attack him now, which meant he could relax more.

It, however, didn't stop Sasha and Bec from talking smack. "We're gonna need to find another job now that the boss has gone soft."

"I know, right?" A bitched agreement. "How are we supposed to hone up on our skills when we're singing 'Kumbaya'?"

"Maybe we could tell him someone insulted you," Bec suggested to Sasha.

"Tell him they insulted Annie and Kay. Then he's sure to snap."

He would have, and he understood their confusion. He had a family now. Responsibilities. But that didn't mean his loyal bodyguards should suffer, which was why when Mab contacted him and told him what she required as payment, he sent Sasha and Bec, along with Callum, to Alaska of all places. Apparently, someone found a door inside a mine they were excavating. A locked door hidden far underground that Mab wanted to know more about.

He might have felt a little jealous at what they might discover, except he'd found everything he ever needed. Family and love.

As if feeling his warm regard, arms slid around him from behind, and Kay's voice purred by his ear. "Have you found a nanny good enough to do the job yet?"

He turned and dropped to his haunches that he might press his face against her swollen belly. "I'm working on it."

Working on living his best life.

---

A FEW WEEKS LATER, a half a world away, Callum stood in front of a door. An ancient portal, covered in sigils that chilled him to the bone.

"I don't think we should open it," he said.

"I agree." Sasha backed him.

"Oops," was Bec's reply as something clicked and the door unlocked.

### THE END...?

Or should I write *The Bear's Job*? Depends on you. To see this series continue, show it some love. Or dive into some more books, at EveLanglais.com

33469287R00095